Marion Lennox was born on an Australian dairy farm. She moved on—mostly because the cows weren't interested in her stories! Marion writes for the Medical Romance™ and Harlequin Romance® lines. Initially she used different names, so, in order to find past books, readers also need to search for author Trisha David. In her non-writing life, Marion cares (haphazardly) for her husband, kids, dogs, cats, chickens, and anyone else who lines up at her dinner table. She fights her rampant garden (she's losing) and her house dust (she's lost!). She also travels, which she finds seriously addictive. As a teenager Marion was told she'd never get anywhere reading romance. Now romance is the basis of her stories, and her stories allow her to travel. If ever there was one advertisement for following your dream, she'd be it! You can contact Marion at www.marionlennox.com.

MARION LENNOX
The Prince's Outback Bride

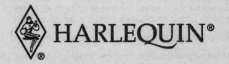

HARLEQUIN®

TORONTO • NEW YORK • LONDON
AMSTERDAM • PARIS • SYDNEY • HAMBURG
STOCKHOLM • ATHENS • TOKYO • MILAN • MADRID
PRAGUE • WARSAW • BUDAPEST • AUCKLAND

ISBN-13: 978-0-373-03950-0
ISBN-10:   0-373-03950-6

THE PRINCE'S OUTBACK BRIDE

First North American Publication 2007.

www.eHarlequin.com

Printed in U.S.A.

There was that smile.

Only it changed every time he used it, she thought. He was like a chameleon, fitting to her moods. Using his smile to make her insides do strange things.

Pippa tugged her hands away—which took some doing—and returned to her place at the table with what she hoped was a semblance of dignity. "Everything's fine."

But everything wasn't fine. Everything was...odd. Max was still smiling as he ladled her pie without being asked.

Her insides felt funny.

It was hunger, she told herself.

She knew it was no such thing.

PROLOGUE

'WE HAVE no choice.' Princess Charlotte de Gautier watched her son in concern from where she rested on her day-bed. Max was pacing the sitting room overlooking the Champs-Elysées. He'd been pacing for hours.

'We must,' Charlotte added bleakly. 'It's our responsibility.'

'It's not our responsibility. The royal family of Alp d'Estella has been rotten to the core for generations. We're well rid of them.'

'They've been corrupt,' Charlotte agreed. 'But now we have the chance to make amends.'

'Amends? Until Crown Prince Bernard's death I thought I had nothing to do with them. Our connection was finished. After all they've done to you...'

'We're not making amends to the royal family. We're making amends to the people of Alp d'Estella.'

'Alp d'Estella's none of our business.'

'That's not true, Max. I'm telling you. It's your birthright.'

'It's not my birthright,' he snapped. 'Regardless of what you say now. It should have been Thiérry's birthright, but their corruption killed Thiérry as it came close to killing you. As far as anyone knows I'm the illegitimate son of the ex-wife of a dead prince. I can walk away. We both can.'

Charlotte flinched. She should have braced herself earlier for this. She'd hoped so much that Crown Prince Bernard would have a son, but now he'd died, leaving...Max.

Since he was fifteen Max had shouldered almost the entire burden of caring for her, and he'd done it brilliantly. But now... She'd tried her hardest to keep her second son out of the royal spotlight—out of the succession—but now it seemed there was no choice but to land at least the regency squarely on Max's shoulders.

Max did a few more turns. Finally he paused and stared down into the bustling Paris street. How could his mother ask this of him—or of herself for that matter? He had no doubt as to what this would mean to their lives. To put Charlotte in the limelight again, as the mother of the Prince Regent…

'I do have a responsibility,' Max said heavily. 'It's to you. To no one else.'

'You know that's not true. You have the fate of a country in your hands.'

'That's not fair.'

'No,' Charlotte whispered. 'Life's not.'

He turned then. 'I'm sorry. Hell, Mama, I didn't mean…'

'I know you didn't. But this has to be faced.'

'But you've given up so much to keep me out of the succession, and to calmly give in now…'

'I'm not giving in. I admit nothing. I'll take the secret of your birth to the grave. I shouldn't have told you, but it seems…so needful that you take on the regency. And it may yet not happen at all. If this child can't become the new Crown Prince…'

'Then what? Will you want to tell the truth then?'

'No,' she said bluntly. 'I will not let you take the Crown.'

'But you'd let an unknown child take it.'

'That's what I mean,' she said, almost eagerly. 'He's an unknown. With no history of hatred weighing him down…maybe it's the only chance for our country.'

'Our country?'

'I still think of it as ours,' she said heavily. 'I might have been a child bride, but I learned early to love it as my own. I love the people. I love the language. I love everything about it. Except its rulers. That's why… That's why I need you to accept the regency. You can help this little prince. I know the politicians. I know the dangers and through you we can protect him. Max, all I know is that we must help him. If you don't take on the regency then the politicians will take over. Things will get worse rather than better, and that's surely saying something.' She hesitated, but it had to be said. 'The way I see it we have two choices. You accept the regency and we do our best to protect this child and protect the people of Alp d'Estella. Or we walk away and let the country self-destruct.'

'And the third alternative?' he asked harshly. 'The truth?'

'No. After all I've been through… You don't want it and I couldn't bear it.'

'No,' he agreed. 'I'm sorry. Of course not.'

'Thank you,' she whispered. 'But what to do now? You tell me this boy's an orphan? That doesn't mean that he's friendless. Who's to say whoever's caring for him will let him take it on?'

'I've made initial enquiries. His registered guardian is a family friend—no relation at all. She's twenty-eight and seems to have been landed with the boy when his parents were killed. This solution provides well for him. She may be delighted to get back to her own life.'

'I guess it's to provide well for him—to let him take on the Crown at such an age. With you beside him…'

'In the background, Mama. From a distance. I can't take anything else on, regardless of what you ask.' Max shoved his hands deep in the pockets of his chinos and, turning, stared once more into the street. Accepting what he'd been thinking for the last hour. 'Maybe he'll be the first decent ruler the country's had for centuries. He can hardly be worse than what's come before. But you're right. We can't let him do it alone. I'll remain caretaker ruler until this child turns twenty-one.'

'You won't live there?'

'No. If there wasn't this family connection stipulation to the regency then I'd never have been approached. But Charles Mevaille's been here this morning—Charles must have been the last non-corrupt politician in the country before the Levouts made it impossible for him to stay. He's shown me what desperately needs to be done to get the country working. The law's convoluted but it seems, no matter who my father was, as half-brother to the last heir I can take on the regency. As Prince Regent I can put those steps into place from here.'

'And the child…'

'We'll employ a great nanny. I'll work hard on that, Mama. He'll be brought up in the castle with everything he could wish for.'

'But…' Charlotte hugged Hannibal—her part poodle, part mongrel, all friend—as if she needed the comfort of Hannibal's soft coat. As indeed she did. 'This is dreadful,' she whispered. 'To put a child in this position…'

'He's an orphan, Mama,' Max said heavily. 'I have no idea what his circumstances are in Australia, but you're right. Once Alp d'Estella's run well then this may well be a glorious opportunity for him.'

'To be wealthy?' Charlotte whispered. 'To be famous? Max, I thought I'd raised you better than that.'

He turned back to face her then, contrite. 'Of course you did. But as far as I can see, this child has no family—only a woman who probably doesn't want to be doing the caring anyway. If she wants to stay with him then we can make it worth her while to come. If she doesn't, then we'll scour the land for the world's best nanny.'

'But you will stay here?'

'I can't stay in Alp d'Estella. Neither of us can.'

'Neither of us have the courage?'

'Mama…'

'You're right,' she said bleakly. 'We don't have the courage, or I surely don't. Let's hope this little one can be what we can't be.'

'We'll care for him,' Max assured her.

'From a distance.'

'It'll be okay.'

'But you will take on the role as Prince Regent?' She sighed. 'I'm so sorry, Max. That's thirteen years of responsibility.'

'As you say, we don't have a choice. And it could have been much, much worse.'

'If I hadn't lied… But I won't go back on it, Max. I won't.'

'No one's asking you to,' he told her, crossing to her day-bed and stooping to kiss her. 'It'll be fine.'

'As long as this woman lets the child come.'

'Why wouldn't she?'

'Maybe she has more sense than I did forty years ago.'

'You were young,' he told her. 'Far too young to marry.'

'So how old is old enough to marry?' she demanded, momentarily distracted.

'Eighty maybe?' He smiled, but the smile didn't reach his eyes. 'Or never. Marriage has never seemed anything but a frightful risk. How the hell would you ever know you weren't being married for your money or your title?' He shrugged. 'Enough. Let's get things moving. We have three short weeks to get things finalised.'

'You'll go to Australia?'

'I can do it from here.'

'You'll go to Australia.' She was suddenly decisive. 'This is a huge thing we're asking.'

'We're relieving this woman of her responsibility.'

'Maybe,' Charlotte whispered. 'But we might just find a woman of integrity. A woman who doesn't think money or a title is an enticement, either for herself or for a child she loves. Now wouldn't that be a problem?'

CHAPTER ONE

A TRUCK had sunk in front of his car.

Wasn't Australia supposed to be a sunburned country? Maxsim de Gautier, Prince Regent of Alp d'Estella, had only been in Australia for six hours, but his overwhelming impression was that the country was fast turning into an inland sea.

But at least he'd found the farm, even though it wasn't what he'd expected. He'd envisaged a wealthy property, but the surrounding land was rough and stony. The farm gate he'd turned into had a faded sign hanging from the top bar reading 'Dreamtime'. In the pouring rain and in such surroundings the name sounded almost defiant.

And now he could drive no further. There was some sort of cattle-grid across the track leading from road to house. The grid had given way and a battered truck was stranded, halfway across.

That meant he'd have to walk the rest of the way. Or swim.

He could sit here until the rain stopped.

It might never stop. The Mercedes he'd hired was luxurious enough but he'd been driving for five hours and flying for twenty-four hours before that, and he didn't intend to sit here any longer.

Was there a back entrance to the farm? There must be if this truck was perpetually blocking the entrance. He rechecked the map supplied by the private investigators he'd employed to locate the child, but the map supplied him with one entrance only.

He'd come too far to let rain come between him and his goal. He'd have to get wet. Dammit, he shouldn't need to, he thought, his sense of humour reasserting itself. Wasn't royalty supposed to have minions who'd lie prone in puddles to save their prince from wet feet?

Where was a good minion when you needed one?

Nowhere. And he wasn't royalty, at least not royalty from the right side of the blanket.

Meanwhile it was a really dumb place to leave a truck. He pushed open the Mercedes door and was met with a deluge. The hire-car contained an umbrella but it was useless in such a torrent. He was soaked before the door was fully open, and the sleet almost blinded him. Nevertheless he turned purposefully towards the house. It was tricky stumbling over the cattle-grid, but he pushed on, glancing sideways into the truck as he passed.

And stopped. Stunned. It wasn't empty. The truck was a two-by-two seater and the back windows were fogged. The back seat seemed to be filled but he couldn't make out what was there. But he could see the front seat. There were six eyes looking out at him—eyes belonging to a woman and a child and a vast brown dog draped over the woman's knee. He stared in at them and they stared back, seemingly as stunned as he was.

This must be the Phillippa the investigators had talked of. But she was…different? The photograph he'd seen, found in a hunt of university archives, had been taken ten years ago. He'd studied it before he'd come. She was attractive, he'd decided, but not in the classic sense. The photograph had showed a smattering of freckles. Her burnt-red curls had looked as if they refused to be tamed. She was curvy rather than svelte, and her grin was more infectious than it was classically lovely. She and Gianetta had been at a university ball. The dress she'd been wearing had been simple, but it had had class.

But now… He recognised the freckles and the dusky red curls, but the face that looked at him was that of a woman who'd left the girl behind. Her face was gaunt, with huge shadows under her eyes. She looked as if she needed to sleep for a long, long time.

And the boy beside her? He had to be Marc. He was a black-haired, brown-eyed kid, dressed in a too-big red and yellow football guernsey. He looked as if he'd just had a growth spurt, skinny and all arms and legs.

He looked like Thiérry, Max thought, stunned. He looked like a de Gautier.

Max dredged up the memory of the report presented to him by the private investigators he'd hired before he came. 'The boy's guardian is Phillippa Donohue. They live on the farm in South Western Victoria that was owned by the boy's parents before they were killed in a car crash four years ago. We've done a preliminary check on the woman but there's not much to report. She qualified as a nurse but she hasn't practised for four years. Her university records state that her mother died when she was twelve. She went through university on a means-tested scholarship and you don't get one of those in Australia if there's any money. As to her circumstances now… We'd need to visit and find out, but it's a tiny farming community and anyone asking questions is bound to be noticed.'

So he knew little except this woman, as Marc's guardian, stood between him and what the people of Alp d'Estella needed.

He didn't know where to start.

She started. She reached over and wound the window a scant inch down so she could talk to him. Any lower and the rain would blast through and make the occupants of the truck as wet as he was.

'Are you out of your mind?' she demanded. 'You'll drown.'

This was hardly a warm welcome. Maybe she could invite him into the truck, he thought, but only fleetingly for it wasn't an option. Opening the door would mean they'd all be soaked.

'Where are you headed?' she asked. She obviously thought he'd stopped to ask directions. As she would. Visitors wouldn't make it here unless they badly wanted to come, and even then they were likely to miss the place. All he'd seen so far were sodden cows, the cattle-grid in which this truck was stuck, and a battered milkcan that obviously served as a mail box, stuck onto a post beside the gate. Fading lettering painted on the side said 'D & G Kettering'.

D & G Kettering. The G would be Gianetta.

It was four years since Gianetta and her husband had died. He'd have expected the sign to be down by now.

What was this woman doing here? Hell, the agency had given him so little information. 'Frankly we can see no reason why Ms Donohue is there,' they'd said. 'We suspect the farm must be substantial, giving her financial incentive to stay. We assume, however, that eventually the farm will belong to the boy, so there's no security in her position. Given her situation, we suspect any approach by you to take responsibility will be welcome.'

They weren't right about the farm being substantial. This farm looked impoverished.

He needed to tread carefully while he found out what the agency hadn't.

'I was searching for the Kettering farm,' he told her. 'I'm assuming this is it? Are you Phillippa Donohue?'

'I'm Pippa, yes.' Her face clouded. 'Are you from the dairy corporation? You've stopped buying our milk. You've stopped our payments. What else can you stop?'

'I'm not from the dairy corporation.'

She stared. 'Not?'

'I came to see you.'

'No one comes to see me.'

'Well, the child,' he told her. 'I'm Marc's cousin.'

She looked out at him, astonished. He wasn't appearing to advantage, he thought, but then, maybe he didn't need to. He just needed to say what had to be said, organise a plane ticket—or plane tickets if she wanted to come—and leave.

'The children don't have cousins,' she said, breaking into his thoughts with a brusqueness that hinted of distrust. 'Gina and Donald—their parents—were both only children. All the grandparents are dead. There's a couple of remote relations on their father's side, but I know them. There's no one else.'

But he'd been caught by her first two words. The children, he thought, puzzled. Children? There was only Marc. Wasn't there?

'I'm a relation on Marc's mother's side,' he said, buying time.

'Gina was my best friend since childhood. Her mother, Alice, was kind to me and I spent lots of time with them. I've never met any relations.'

She sounded so suspicious that he smiled. 'So you think I'm with the dairy corporation, trying to sneak into your farm with lies about my family background? You think I'd risk drowning to talk to an unknown woman about *cows*?'

She stared some more, and slowly the corners of her mouth curved into an answering smile. Suddenly the resemblance to the old photograph was stronger. He saw for the first time why his initial impression from the photograph had been beauty.

'I guess that would be ridiculous,' she conceded. 'But you're not their cousin.'

Their cousin. There it was again. Plural. He didn't understand, so he ploughed on regardless. 'I am a relation. Gianetta and I shared a grandfather—not that we knew him. I've come from half a world away to see Marc.'

'You're from the royal part of the family?' she said, sounding as if she'd suddenly remembered something she'd been told long since.

He winced. 'Um…maybe. I need to talk to you. I need to see Marc.'

'You're seeing him,' she said unhelpfully.

He looked at Marc. Marc looked back, wary now because he wasn't understanding the conversation. He'd edged slightly in front of Pippa in a gesture of protection.

He was so like the de Gautiers it unnerved Max.

'Hi,' he told Marc. 'I'd like to talk to you.'

'We're not in a situation where visits are possible,' she said, and her arm came around Marc's skinny chest. They were protecting each other. But she sounded intrigued now, and there was even a tinge of regret in her voice. 'Do you need a bed for the night?'

This was hopeful. 'I do.'

'There's a guesthouse in Tanbarook. Come back in the morning after milking. We'll give you a cup of coffee and find the time to talk.'

'Gee, thanks.'

Her smile broadened. 'I'm sorry, but it's the best I can do. We're a bit…stuck at the moment. Now, you need to find Tanbarook. Head back to the end of this road and turn right. That's a sealed road which will get you into town.'

'Thanks,' he said but he didn't go. They were gazing at him, Marc with curiosity and slight defensiveness, Pippa with calm friendliness and the dog with the benign observance of a very old and very placid mutt. Pippa was reaching over to wind up the window. 'Don't,' he told her.

'Don't?'

'Why are you sitting in a truck in the middle of a cattle pit?'

'We're stuck.'

'I can see that. How long do you intend to sit here?'

'Until the rain stops.'

'This rain,' he said cautiously, 'may never stop.' He grimaced as a sudden squall sent a rush of cold water down the back of his neck. More and more he felt like a drowned rat. Heaven knew what Pippa would be thinking of him. Not much, he thought.

That alone wasn't what he was used to. Women normally reacted strongly to Maxsim de Gautier. He was tall and strongly built, with the Mediterranean skin, deep black hair and dark features of his mother's family. The tabloids described him as drop-dead gorgeous and seriously rich.

But Pippa could see little of this and guess less. She obviously didn't have a clue who he was. Maybe she could approximate his age—thirty-five—but it'd be a wild guess. Mostly she'd be seeing water.

'Forty days and forty nights is the rain record,' he told her. 'I think we're heading for that now.'

She smiled. 'So if I were you I'd get back in your car and head for dry land.'

'Why didn't you go back to the house instead of waiting here in the truck?'

Until now Marc had stayed silent, watching him with wariness. But now the little boy decided to join in.

'We're going to get fish and chips,' he informed him. 'But the cattle-grid broke so we're stuck. We have to wait 'til it stops raining. Then we have to find Mr Henges and ask him to pull us out with his tractor. Pippa says we might as well sit here and whinge 'cos it's warmer here than in the house. We've run out of wood.'

'The gentleman doesn't need to know why we're sitting here,' Pippa told him.

'But we've been sitting here for ages and we're hungry.'

'Shh.'

Marc, however, was preparing to be sociable. 'I'm Marc and this is our Pippa and this is our dog, Dolores. And over the back is Sophie and Claire. Sophie has red hair ribbons and Claire's are blue.'

Sophie and Claire. Over the back. He peered through the tiny slot of wound-down window. Yes, there were two more children. He could make out two little faces, with similar colouring to Marc. Cute and pigtailed. Red and blue ribbons. Twins?

Sophie and Claire. He hadn't heard of any Sophie and Claire. Were they Pippa's? But they looked like Marc. And Pippa had red hair.

No matter. It was only Marc he needed to focus on. 'I'm pleased to meet you all,' he said. This was a crazy place to have a conversation, but he had to start introductions some time. 'I'm Max.'

'Hi,' Pippa said and put her hand on the window winder again. Dismissing him. 'Good luck. We may see you tomorrow.'

'Can't I help you?'

'We're fine.'

'I could tow you.'

'Do you have a tow-bar on your car?'

'Um…no.' It was a hire-car—a luxury saloon. Of course he didn't. 'Can I find Mr Henges and his tractor for you?'

'Bert won't come 'til the rain stops.'

'You're planning on sitting in the truck until then?'

'Or until it's time for milking.'

The thought of milking cows in this weather didn't bear considering. 'You don't think maybe you could run back to the house, peel off your wet things, have a hot shower and…oh, I don't know, play Happy Families until milking?'

'It's warmer here,' Marc said.

'But we want fish and chips,' one of the little girls piped up from the back seat.

'There's bread,' Marc said, in severe, big-brother tones. 'We'll make toast before milking.'

'We want fish and chips,' the other little girl whimpered. 'We're hungry.'

'Shh.' Pippa turned back to Max. 'Can you move away so I can wind up the window? We're getting wet.'

'Sure.' But Max didn't move. He thought of all he'd come to say to this woman and he winced. Back home it had seemed simple—to say what needed to be said and walk away. But now, suddenly, it seemed harder. 'Isn't there anything I can do for you first?'

What was he saying? The easiest thing to do right now would be to walk away from the whole mess, he thought. Someone else could tell these people what they had to know. But then, he'd have to remember that he'd walked away for a long time.

'We don't need anything,' Pippa told him, oblivious to his train of thought, and he dragged his attention back to the matter at hand. Truck stuck. Fish and chips.

'I'm thinking I should talk to Marc about this,' he said, focusing on food. 'This is, after all, men's business. Hunting and gathering. You were heading to the shops when your truck got stuck. Looking for fish and chips.'

'Yes,' said Marc, pleased at his acuity, and Sophie and Claire beamed agreement, anticipating assistance. 'We've run out of food,' Marc told him. 'All we have left is toast. We don't even have any jam.'

Right. He could do this. Jam and fish and chips. But not drowned like this.

'I have a car that's not stuck in a cattle-grid,' he told them. 'But I'm soaking wet. You have a house where I can dry off, and I've come a long way to visit you. Let's combine. You let me use your house to change and I'll go into town and buy fish and chips.'

'We can't impose on you,' Pippa said. But she looked desperate, and he wondered why.

First things first. He had to persuade her to let him help. 'I'm not an axe murderer,' he told her. 'I promise. I really am a relation.'

'But…'

'I'm Maxsim de Gautier. Max.' He watched to see if there was recognition of the name, but she was too preoccupied to think of anything but immediate need—and maybe she'd never heard the name anyway. 'I'd really like to help.'

Desperation faded—just a little. 'I shouldn't let you.'

'Yes, you should. You don't have to like me, but I'm definitely family, so you need to sigh and open the door, the way most families ask rum-soaked Uncle Bertie or similar to Christmas lunch.'

She smiled in return at that, a wobbly sort of smile but it was a welcome change from the desperate. 'Uncle Bertie or similar?'

'I'm not even a soak,' he said encouragingly and her smile wobbled a bit more.

'You have a great accent,' she said inconsequentially. 'It sounds…familiar. Is it Italian or French?'

'Mostly French.'

'You're very wet.'

'The puddle around my ankles is starting to creep to my knees. If you leave this decision much longer I'll need a snorkel.'

She stared out at him and chewed her lip. Then she seemed to make a decision. 'Fine.'

'Fine what?'

'Fine I'll trust you,' she managed. 'The kids and I will trust you, but I'm not sure about Dolores.' She hugged the dog tighter. 'She bites relations who turn out to be axe murderers.'

'She's welcome to try. How will we organise this?'

'My truck's blocking your way to the house.'

'So it is,' he said cordially. 'Why didn't I notice that?'

Her decision meant that she'd relaxed a little. The lines of strain around her eyes had eased. Now she even choked back a bubble of laughter. 'We need to run to the house. We'll all be soaked the minute we get out of the truck.'

'I assume you have dry clothes back at the house?'

'Yes but…'

'I'm bored of sitting in the truck,' Marc said.

'Me too,' said Sophie.

'Me too,' said Claire.

'Right,' Pippa said, coming to a decision. 'On the count of three I want everybody out of the truck and we'll run back to the house as fast as we can. Mr de Gautier, you're welcome to follow.'

'I'll do backstroke,' he told her. 'What's your stroke?'

'Dog-paddle.' She pushed open the driver's side door and dived into the torrent. 'Okay, kids,' she said, hauling open the back door and starting to lift them out.

'Let me,' he told her.

'I'll take the kids. You take Dolores.'

'Dolores?'

'She hates getting her feet wet,' Pippa explained. 'She's had pneumonia twice so she has an excuse. I'll carry her if I must but I have a sore back and as you're here I don't see why you shouldn't be useful. After all, you are family.'

'Um…okay,' he managed, but that was all he could say before a great brown dog of indiscriminate parentage was pushed out of the cab and into his arms.

'Don't drop her,' Pippa ordered. 'And run.'

'Yes, ma'am.'

The house was two hundred yards from the gate, and, even though they ran fast, by the time they reached it they were all sodden. Max's first impression was that it was a rambling weatherboard house, a bit down at heel, but it was unfair to judge when he saw everything through sleeting rain. And over one dog who smelled like…wet dog.

There was a veranda. Marc led the way. Pippa ran up the steps behind him, holding a twin by each hand. Max and Dolores brought up the rear. He'd paused to grab his holdall from his car, so he was balancing dog and holdall. Where were those servile minions? he thought again. Maybe accepting the crown could have its uses.

He wasn't going there, minions or not. He reached the top step, set Dolores down, tossed his holdall into the comparative dry at the back of the veranda, mourned his minions for another fleeting moment, and then turned his attention to the little family before him.

At eight, Marc was just doing the transformation from cute into kid. Maybe he was tall for his age, Max thought, but what did he know about kids? He had the same jet black curls all the members of the Alp d'Estella royal family had, and big brown eyes and a snub nose with a smattering of freckles.

Sophie and Claire were different but similar. They were still not much more than tots, with glossy black curls tied into pigtails and adorned with bright ribbons that now hung limply down their back. They were cute and well rounded and they had a whole lot more freckles than their brother did.

They had to be Marc's sisters, Max thought, cursing his PI firm for their lack of information. But then, what had his brief been? Find Marc and report on where he was living and who was taking care of him. Nothing about sisters.

But surely the powers that be back in Alp d'Estella must know of these two? They'd certainly known of Marc.

Marc was drying himself, towelling his face with vigour. The twins were being towelled by Pippa. All three children were regarding him cautiously from under their towels.

They were bright, inquisitive kids, he thought. Pippa said something to them and they giggled.

Nice kids.

He shouldn't stare.

Pippa was stripping off the girls' outer clothes. She tossed him a towel from a pile by the door. He started to dry his face but was brought up short.

'That's for Dolores.'

'Sorry?' He looked blank and she sighed.

'Dolores. Pneumonia. Prevention of same. Please can you rub?'

'Um…sure.' He knelt as she was kneeling but instead of undressing kids he was towelling dog. Dolores approved. She rubbed herself ecstatically against the towel, and when he turned her to do the front half she showed her appreciation by giving him a huge lick, from his chin to his forehead. She was big and all bone—a cross between a Labrador and something even bigger. A bloodhound? In dog years she looked about a hundred.

'She's kissing you,' four-year-old Sophie said, and giggled. 'That means she likes you.'

'I've had better kisses in my day,' he said darkly.

'Let's not go there, Cousin Max,' Pippa muttered. 'Otherwise I'll think axe again.'

'No kissing,' Max agreed with alacrity and towelled Dolores harder. 'You hear that, Dolores? Keep yourself respectable or the lady with the axe knows what to do.'

Pippa chuckled. It was a great chuckle, he thought. He towelled

Dolores for a while longer but he was watching Pippa. She was wearing ancient jeans and a windcheater with a rip up one arm. Her close-cropped, coppery curls were plastered wetly to her head, and droplets of rainwater were running down her forehead. She wore no make-up. She'd been wearing huge black wellingtons and she'd kicked them off at the top of the stairs. Underneath she was wearing what looked like football socks. The toe was missing from one yellow and black sock, and her toe poked pinkly through.

Very sexy, he thought, smiling inwardly, but then he glanced at her again and thought actually he was right. She was sexy but she was a very different sort of sexy from the women he normally associated with.

Where was he going with this? Nowhere, he told himself, startled. He was here to organise the succession; nothing more.

The kids were undressed to their knickers now. 'The quickest way to warm is to shower and we'll do it in relays,' Pippa was saying. She motioned to a door at the end of the veranda. 'That's the bathroom. The kids can shower first. Then me. I'm sorry, Mr de Gautier, but in this instance it needs to be visitors last. Stay here until I call. We'll be as quick as we can.'

'What about Dolores?'

'She can go through to the kitchen if she wants,' Pippa said, holding the door open for the dog. 'Though if you really want I guess she could shower with you.' She smiled again, a lovely, laughing smile that made these bleak surroundings seem suddenly brighter. 'Bathing Dolores usually takes a small army, but thanks for offering. Good luck.'

He didn't shower with the dog. Dolores disappeared as soon as the kids did, leaving Max to wait alone on the veranda. Maybe Dolores had a warm kennel somewhere, Max thought enviously as the wind blasted its way through his wet clothes. Wasn't Australia supposed to be warm?

Luckily the kids and Pippa were faster than he expected. Pippa reappeared within five minutes, dressed in a pink bathrobe with her hair tied up in a tattered green towel. She tossed him a towel that wasn't quite as frayed as the one he'd used for Dolores.

'I assume you have dry clothes in your bag,' she said and he nodded.

'Lucky you,' she said. 'Everything here is wet. It's been raining for days. Shower's through there. Enjoy.'

Everything here was wet? Didn't she have a dryer? He thought about that while standing under the vast rose shower hanging over the claw-foot bath in the ancient bathroom. Everything he'd seen so far spoke of poverty. Surely Marc—and the girls?— were well provided for?

Alice, Gianetta's mother, had cut off all ties to her family back in Europe. 'She married well,' he'd been told. 'Into the Australian squattocracy.' But then, that had been his father speaking, and his father treated the truth with disdain.

Up until now Max hadn't been interested to find the truth for himself, but if these children's maternal grandmother had married into money there was nothing to show for it now.

There were questions everywhere. He showered long enough to warm up; he dried; he foraged in his holdall and dressed in chinos and an oversized sweater that he'd almost not packed because Australia was supposed to be warm. Then he set out to find them.

The bathroom led to what looked like a utility room. A door on the far side of the utility room led somewhere else, and he could hear children's voices close by. He pushed it with caution and found himself in the farmhouse kitchen. Here they were, the children in dressing gowns and slippers and Pippa in jeans and another windcheater. The cuffs of her windcheater looked damp, he thought. What had she said? Everything was wet? Where the hell was a dryer? Or a fire of some sort?

The kitchen was freezing.

Pippa and the kids were seated at the table, with steaming mugs before them. Dolores was under the table, lying on a towel.

'Get yourself warm on the inside as well as the outside before we send you off as hunter gatherer,' Pippa said, and she smiled. It was a great smile, he thought, astonishing himself with the intensity of his reaction. In her ancient windcheater and jeans she looked barely older than the kids. The oversized windcheater made her look flat-chested and insignificant. But still it was a killer of a smile. Something inside him reacted when she smiled.

That was a crazy thing to think right now. He needed to figure things out. Too many kids for a start. And this place… Despite the shower and his thick sweater he felt himself starting to shiver. The temperature was as low as outside. Which was pretty low.

'Hot chocolate?' Pippa offered. She was using a small electric cooker top. Beside the cooker top was a much larger stove. An Aga.

They had an Aga and didn't have it lit?

'We don't have wood,' she said, seeing what he was looking at and guessing what he was thinking.

'I know. Marc mentioned it earlier. Why not?'

'Pippa hurt her back,' Marc volunteered. 'So she can't chop wood. There's a dead tree in the far paddock and Pippa cuts it up when we run out but she can't cut any more until her back gets better.'

'What happened to your back?'

'She fell off the roof,' Marc said, sounding severe for his eight years. 'Trying to nail roofing iron back on. I told her she'd fall off and she did.'

'I didn't have much choice,' Pippa said with a trace of defiance. She was talking to Marc as she'd talk to an adult. 'If I hadn't we'd be in water up to our necks right now.'

'It was scary,' Sophie—was Sophie the red ribbons?—informed Max. 'It was really, really windy. Marc was yelling at her to come down.'

'And then some roof came off and she fell,' Claire added, relishing an exciting story. 'Sophie screamed but I didn't and Pippa grabbed the edge of the roof and hung on. And she cut her hand and it bled and we had to put a bandage onto it.'

'I told her not to do it,' Marc muttered darkly.

What was going on here? Guardian and kids, or four kids?

'I won't do it again,' Pippa told Marc, reaching out to ruffle his dark hair. 'It's fixed.' He looked over to Max. 'How are you related to the kids?'

'I believe Marc's grandmother, Alice, was my aunt.'

'I remember Grandma Alice.' Marc nodded. 'She died just before

Mama and Daddy were killed and we were really sad. She said we had royal cousins, but she said they were a bad lot.' He thought about it and drank some of his chocolate. 'I don't know what a bad lot is.'

'I hope I'm not a bad lot.'

'But you're royal. Like a king or something.'

'I'm on the same side of the family as you.'

'Not on the bad lot side?'

'No.'

The girls—and Pippa—were listening to this interchange with various levels of interest. Now Sophie felt the need to interrupt.

'I'm really very hungry,' she said soulfully—martyr about to die a stoic death—and Pippa handed Max his hot chocolate, glanced at Claire who'd gone quiet and made a decision.

'Um...can the family-tree thing wait? If you really are family... Actually we are in a bit of trouble,' she confessed. 'We don't have anything to eat.'

'Nothing?'

'Toast. But no butter. And no jam.'

'You believe in putting off shopping to the last minute.'

'We tried to put it off 'til the rain stopped. But it didn't.'

'I see.' Though he didn't see.

'Could you really go into town and pick up a few supplies?'

'Of course. You could come with me if you like.'

'All of us?' Pippa asked.

He did a quick head count. Maybe...

'Including Dolores.'

He looked down at Dolores—a great brown dog, gently steaming and wafting wet dog smell through the kitchen.

'Maybe I'm fine by myself,' Max said.

She chuckled, a nice chuckle that might have had the capacity to warm the kitchen if it wasn't so appallingly cold. Then she eyed him appraisingly. 'You'll get wet again, walking back to your car. That's not exactly wet-weather gear.'

'Lend him Daddy's milking gear,' Marc piped up. 'He's bigger than Daddy but he might fit.'

'He can wear Daddy's gumboots,' Sophie offered.

'Gumboots?'

'That's Australian for wellingtons,' Pippa said.

'He needs an umbrella,' Claire added. Like all of them she'd been staring at Max with caution, but she'd obviously reached a decision. 'He can use my doggy umbrella.' She fetched it from near the back door, opened it and twirled it for inspection. Pale pink, it had a picture of an appealing puppy on every panel. 'You'll look after it,' she said, as one conferring a huge level of trust.

Great, Max thought. Prince Regents wearing wellingtons and carrying umbrellas with dogs? Thankfully the paparazzi were half a world from here.

There was so much here that he hadn't expected. Actually nothing was what he'd expected. Except Marc. Marc looked just like Max's brother. Which was great. It made things almost perfect.

Except… It made his gut do this lurching kind of thing. A kid who looked like Thiérry…

He glanced at Marc again and Pippa intercepted the look. 'What?'

'Nothing.'

'Why were you looking at Marc?'

'I was wondering why he was dark when you're a redhead.' He knew the relationship but it didn't hurt to check.

'Pippa's not related to us,' Marc told him. 'She's our friend.'

'Pippa's our aunty,' Sophie volunteered, but Marc shook his head.

'No, she's not. She and Mummy were friends and Pippa promised she'll look after us, just like a real aunty. But she's not our real aunty.'

'I wish she was,' Claire whispered.

'I'm just as good as an aunty,' Pippa said stoutly. 'Only bossier. More like a mother hen, really.' She was staring across the table at him as she spoke, her voice…challenging? Max met her look head-on. Had she guessed why he was here?

He had to tell her, but let it come slowly, he thought. It'd be easy to get a blank no, with no room to manoeuvre. Surely the poverty he saw in this place meant he'd at least get a hearing.

Meanwhile… 'Where's this wet-weather gear?'

'I'll show you.' Pippa produced a battered purse and handed over two notes and a couple of coins. 'Our budget for the rest of the week is thirty-two dollars, fifty cents,' she told him. 'Can you buy fish and chips and bread, jam, some dried pasta and a slab of cheap cheese? Spend the change on dog food. The cheapest there is.'

He stared down at the notes and coins in disbelief. 'You're kidding,' he said finally, and she flushed.

'We're momentarily broke,' she admitted. 'Our vats were found to be contaminated. It's only low level—we're still drinking our milk—but it's bad enough to stop sales. We need a week's clear testing before the dairy corporation will buy our milk again.'

'But we can't afford new vats,' Marc interjected. 'Pippa says we're up the creek without a paddle.' He sounded almost cheerful but Max saw Pippa wince and realised there was real distress behind those words.

'That's not Mr de Gautier's problem,' Pippa said, gently reproving. 'But we do have to pull in our belts. Mr de Gautier, I'd appreciate if you could do our buying for us, but that's all we need. We'll be fine.'

'Will you be fine without fruit?' he asked, staring at the list in disapproval. 'What about scurvy?'

'No one gets scurvy if they go without for only a week.'

'No, but…' He searched her face for a long moment, seeing quiet dignity masking a background of desperation. What on earth was she doing here? She seemed to be stuck on an almost derelict farm with three kids who weren't hers and a dog who'd seen better days. The investigators said there was no blood tie. Why hadn't she walked away?

Until now this had seemed easy. He'd expected to be back on a plane by the end of the week. With Marc. Maybe with Pippa as well. It could still happen, but that jutting chin prompted doubts. The little girls prompted more. Plus the way the dog was draped so she was touching everyone's feet.

Enough. He squared his shoulders and accepted an umbrella. Doubts had to wait. He had to go shopping.

CHAPTER TWO

TANBAROOK was tiny. The place consisted of five shops, a pub, two churches and a school. Most of them looked deserted, but there were three cars lined up outside a small supermarket. A Tanbarook crowd, Max thought wryly and went in to join it. He sloshed through the door and four women stared at him as if he'd landed from Mars.

The ladies were at the checkout counter, one behind the register, the others on the customer side. He gave them what he hoped was a pleasant smile. 'Good afternoon.'

'Good afternoon,' four voices chorused.

He grabbed a trolley and turned to the shelves.

'Can I help?' the woman behind the register called.

'I'm fine, thank you. I have a list.'

'Your wife's given you a list?' Heaven knew how long it had been raining, but this group looked as if they'd been propping up the checkout counter for years.

'No,' he said discouragingly, but it didn't work.

'Then who gave you the list?'

'Pippa,' he said, grudgingly.

'Phillippa Donohue?' Four sets of eyes nearly started from four heads. 'The woman on Kettering's farm,' one of them exclaimed. 'I didn't think she had a boyf—'

'He'll be a friend from when she was nursing,' another interrupted, digging her friend in the ribs. 'Maybe he's a doctor.'

Four sets of eyebrows twitched upward and he could almost see the assembling of symptoms. 'Are you a doctor?'

'No.'

Four sets of brows drooped in disappointment, and they turned their backs on him. 'Maybe he's a friend from university,' one said. 'That's where Gina met Donald. He was doing a course on farm bookkeeping. One weekend was all it took for them to fall in love. Wham.'

'Did Phillippa go to university?'

'Of course she did. Nurses have to go to university these days. She went and so did Gina. Not that Gina ever worked as a nurse. She married Donald instead. I remember just after they were married, Phillippa came to visit. Gina was really excited. She said Phillippa was clever. She could have been a doctor, Gina said, but of course there wasn't any money. But she had a really good job. In operating theatres, Gina said. Mind, you wouldn't think she was clever now, holding on to that farm against all odds. Stupid girl.'

The lady giving the information was wearing hair curlers and some sort of shapeless crimplene frock. She had her arms crossed across her ample bosom in the classic stance of 'I know more than you do'. She practically smirked.

'She should go back to nursing,' she told her friends. 'Why she insists on keeping that farm… It's just an impediment, that's what it is.'

'But she likes the farm,' another objected. 'She told me so. That's why she won't sell.'

'Honestly, would anyone like that dump? And she's standing in the way of progress.'

'She says it feels like home.'

'It might be the children's home,' Crimplene conceded. 'But if Phillippa wasn't there they'd be put up for adoption. Which would probably be for the best, and the sooner she admits it, the better. They'll be starving soon.'

'But if she's got a boyfriend…' They turned as one to inspect him again. 'If she's got a boyfriend then maybe she'll have support.' It didn't seem to be an idea they relished.

'You're French,' one of them said, obviously replaying his voice and discovering the accent.

'No.' He might be interested in what they had to say about Pippa, but the last thing he wanted was an inquisition about himself. He redirected his attention to his list. Bread, pasta, dog food. Ha. And the thirty-two dollars and fifty cents had to be a joke. Good coffee was eight dollars a pack. Three packs, he decided, and tossed in another for good measure.

What next? Tea? Surely. And the kids really should have decent hot chocolate—not the watered-down stuff they were drinking now. If Marc was to end up where he hoped, it was time he learned to appreciate quality. He found tubs of chocolate curls with pictures of decadent mugs of creaming hot chocolate on the front. Two tubs landed in his trolley.

He'd turned his back on his audience. They didn't like it.

'Phillippa can't afford that,' the lady behind the checkout snapped. 'Her vats are contaminated.'

'My vats aren't,' he retorted, inspecting the range of chocolate cookies and choosing four packets before moving on to confectionery. What was hot chocolate without marshmallows? Would six packets be enough?

Then there were more decisions. Did they like milk chocolate or dark? Three blocks of each, he decided, but the blocks looked a bit small. Okay, six of each.

On then to essentials. Dry pasta. Surely she wasn't serious about wanting much of this. It looked so…dry. The meat section looked much more appetising. The steaks looked great.

But then, this wasn't just about him, he reminded himself. The steaks looked wonderful, but maybe kids liked sausages. He replaced a couple of steaks, collected sausages, and then thought of Dolores and the great big eyes. He put the steaks back in his trolley.

Then he discovered the wine section. Australian wine. Excellent. And fruit? He wasn't as sure as Pippa about the scurvy

thing. That meant fresh produce. Bananas. Oranges. Strawberries? Of course strawberries. Would they have their own
cream or should he buy some?

But there was more to shopping than food.

'I need wood,' he said, and discovered the ladies were staring
at his trolley as if they'd never seen such things. 'Where can I
find fuel for a woodstove?'

'You can't cut wood in weather like this.'

'That's the problem,' he said patiently. 'And Pippa has a bad
back.'

'We know that,' one of the ladies said, starting to sound
annoyed. 'She hurt it last week. The doctor told her to be careful.
I expect all her fires are out by now.' She sounded smug.

'They are,' Max said shortly. 'No locals thought to help her?'

'She's not a local herself,' another of the ladies said, doubtfully now, maybe considering that they might be considered
remiss. 'She only came here when the children's parents died.
And she won't sell the farm. We all tell her she should sell the
farm. It's a huge problem for the district.'

'Why?'

'We want to put a new road in. There's ten outlying farms—
huge concerns—that have three miles or more to get into town.
If Phillippa agreed to sell her place we could build a bridge over
the creek. It'd be a lot more convenient for everyone.'

'I see,' he said slowly. 'Would that be why her vats have been
found to be contaminated?'

'Of course not,' Crimplene snapped, but she flushed. 'But it's
nothing more than we expected. She has some stupid idea of
keeping the farm for the children. As if she can ever keep it as a
going concern until they're adult. It's ridiculous.'

'So she doesn't qualify for help when she's hurt?' He caught
himself then. What was the use of being angry—and what
business was it of his? Pippa was nothing to do with him. He just
needed to do what he had to do and move on.

It was just she looked so…slight. David against Goliath. Or
Pippa against Crimplene. He'd prefer to take on Goliath any
day, he thought. Crimplene made him feel ill.

'Where can I buy some wood to tide us over?' he said, trying very hard to keep anger out of his voice.

'We have barbecue packs,' the checkout lady said. She also seemed unsure, casting a nervous glance at Crimplene as if she was bucking an agreed plan. 'We sell them to tourists at a big... I mean for premium prices. There's ten logs per bundle at five dollars a bundle.'

Max thought back to the enormous woodstove and he thought of Pippa's fingers, tinged with blue from the cold. He looked at the four women in front of him. They stared straight back and he felt the anger again. Sure, he was a stranger, and it was none of his business, but he remembered the shadows under Pippa's eyes and he couldn't stop being angry.

Anger achieved nothing, he told himself. He was here on a mission. He had to focus.

'How many bundles do you have in stock?' he asked.

'Forty maybe.'

'If I buy them all will you deliver?'

There was a general gasp. 'That's wicked waste,' Crimplene started but the checkout lady was seeing dollars.

'Sure we will,' she said. 'When do you want them?'

'You can't,' Crimplene gasped but the checkout lady was looking at a heady profit.

'Now,' Max told her.

'I'll get hubby from the back,' she said, breathless. 'For that amount Duncan can get his backside off the couch and I don't care if it is against what you want, Doreen. Your precious road can wait. It's uncivilised, what you're doing to that family, and I don't mind who I say it to.' Then as Crimplene's bosom started to swell in indignation she smiled at Max and gazed lovingly at the very expensive produce in his trolley. 'Do you want me to ring these through?'

'Not yet,' Max said, moving further down the aisle, away from the women he wanted suddenly—stupidly—to lash out at. Pippa was to be neglected no longer, he thought. If he bought the entire store out and the population of Tanbarook went hungry because of it, then so much the better. Vengeance by Commerce. He almost managed a smile. 'I've hardly started.'

'Go tell Duncan to start loading wood,' he told the ladies. 'Now do you know where I can buy fish and chips? Oh, and a clothes dryer?'

'He'll probably abscond with my thirty-two dollars and fifty cents.'

Back at the farmhouse, the kids and Dolores were out on the veranda waiting for Max's return and Pippa was starting to think she'd been a dope. What if he never came back? She hadn't even taken the registration number of his car.

Who was he?

Max de Gautier. The royal side of the family.

Pippa smiled at that, remembering Gianetta's pleasure in her royal background. Alice, Gina's mother, had tried to play it down, but Gianetta had been proud of it.

'My great-uncle is the Crown Prince of Alp d'Estella,' she'd tell anyone who'd listen. After the old prince died, she'd had to change her story to: 'I'm related to the Crown Prince of Alp d'Estella.' It didn't sound as impressive, but she'd still enjoyed saying it.

But it meant nothing. When Alice died there'd been no call from royalty claiming kinship. Gina had married her Australian dairy farmer, and, storytelling aside, she'd considered herself a true Australian. Royalty might have sounded fun but it hadn't been real. Her beloved Donald had been real.

Marc came in then, searching for reassurance that Max would indeed return.

'I don't know why he's so long,' Pippa told him, and then hesitated. 'Marc, you remember your mama showed us a family tree of the royal family she said you were related to?'

'Mmm,' Marc said. 'Grandma drew it for us. I couldn't read it then but I can now. It's in my treasure box.'

'Can we look at it?'

So they did. The tree that Alice had drawn was simple, first names only, wives or husbands, drawn in neat handwriting with a little childish script added later.

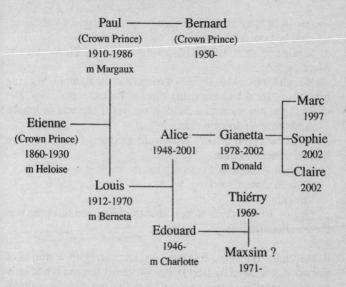

Marc spread it out on the kitchen table and both of them studied it. Marc was an intelligent little boy, made old beyond his years by the death of his parents. Sometimes Pippa thought she shouldn't talk to him as an equal, but then who else could she talk to?

'I wrote the twins and two thousand and two and stuff when I learned to write,' Marc said and Pippa hugged him and kept reading.

'Etienne was your great-great-grandfather,' she told him, following the line back. 'Look, there's Max. His grandpa and your great-grandfather were the same. Louis. I guess Louis must have been a prince.'

'Why aren't I a prince?'

'Because your grandma was a girl?' she said doubtfully. 'I think princes' kids are princes but princesses' kids aren't.' She hesitated and then admitted: 'Actually, Marc, I'm not sure.'

Marc followed the lines himself, frowning in concentration. 'Why is there a question mark beside Max's name?'

'I don't know.'

'Is Max a prince?'

'He didn't say he was a prince.'

'It'd be cool if he was.'

'I hope he's not. I don't have a tiara to wear,' Pippa said and Marc giggled.

Which Pippa liked. He was too serious, she thought, hugging him close. He'd had too many dramas for one small boy. She should treat him more as a child. It was just…she was so lonely.

And thinking about it didn't help.

'Will he come back?' Marc said anxiously and she gave herself a mental shake.

'Of course he will. I'll sweep the floor while we wait.'

'You're always working.'

'Working's fun.'

Or not. But working stopped her thinking, and thinking was the harsher alternative.

Max finally returned, followed by Duncan with a trailer of firewood, followed by Bert Henges with his tractor. It had only taken a promise of cash to get Bert out in the rain. Three men and a tractor made short work of hauling the truck from the pit. They heaved planks over the broken grid and Bert departed—bearing cash—while Duncan and Max drove cautiously across to the house. The kids had been watching from the veranda but as soon as they drove closer they disappeared. Duncan began tossing wood up to Max, who started stacking it next to the back door.

They'd unpacked half a dozen bundles when Pippa emerged. She was holding her broom like a rifle, and the three children were close behind.

She looks cute, Max thought inconsequentially. Defensive—have broom will shoot!—but cute.

'What's going on?' she demanded; then as she saw what they were doing she gasped. 'Where did that come from?'

'My shed,' Duncan said, unaccustomed profits making him cheerful. 'Seems you've got a sugar-daddy, Pippa, love.'

'I do not have a sugar-daddy,' she said, revolted. 'I can't afford this.'

'It's paid for. You've struck a good'un here.' He motioned to Max with a dirty thumb and tossed another bundle.

'Will you cut it out?' She looked poleaxed. 'How did you get the vehicles here?'

'Bert hauled your truck out of the pit.' The wood merchant was obviously relishing enough gossip to keep a dreary country week enlivened until the rain stopped. 'Courtesy of your young man.'

'You didn't get Bert out into the rain?' she demanded of Max, appalled. She stepped into his line of tossing to stop the flow of wood. 'He'll charge a fortune and I can't pay. Of all the stupid… It was just a matter of waiting.'

'You don't need to pay.' Max handed her his bundle of wood. 'I already have. Can you start the fire with this? There are fire-lighters and matches in the grocery sacks. Most of the groceries are in the trunk. I've backed right up so we can unpack without getting wet.'

'Most of the groceries…' She stared at him, speechless, and he placed his hands on her shoulders and put her aside so Duncan could toss him another bundle.

The feel of him…the strength of him… She felt as if she'd been lifted up and transported into another place.

She gasped and tugged away. 'I can't take this,' she managed, staring down into the stuffed-full trunk of his car. There were chocolate cookies spilling out from the sacks. Real coffee!

'Why not? The farmhouse is freezing and it's no part of my plan to have you guys freeze to death.'

'Your plan?'

'My plan,' he said. 'Can you light the fire and we'll talk this through when we're warm?'

She stared blindly at the wood, confusion turning to anger. 'You can't just buy us. I don't understand what you want but you can't have it. We don't want your money.'

'Pippa, I'm family and therefore I have the right to make sure you—or at least the children—are warm and well fed,' he said, gently but firmly. He fielded and stacked another bundle. 'Please. Get the fire lit and then we can talk. Oh, and the fish and chips will be here in fifteen minutes. Home delivery.'

'Home delivery?' she gasped. 'When did they ever…'

'They'd run out of potatoes at the pub,' he said apologetically. 'But Mrs Ryan says Ern can go out and dig some and she'll have fish and chips here by three.'

'I bet he paid her as much as he paid me,' Duncan said cheerfully and he winked at her. 'You're on a winner here, love.'

She stared, open-mouthed, at them both. She couldn't think of a thing to say.

'Light the fire,' Max said—and Pippa stared at him wordlessly for a full minute.

Then she went to light the fire.

It seemed she had no alternative.

She might not like it—well, okay, she liked it but she might not trust it—but he was right; she had no choice but to accept. He was related to the children, which was more than she was.

So she unpacked and as the kids whooped their joy she felt dizzy.

'Sausages,' they shouted, holding each item up for inspection. 'Eggs. We haven't had this many eggs since the fox ate our last chook. Marmalade. Yuck, we don't like marmalade. But there's honey. Honey, honey, honey! And chocolate. More chocolate. Lemonade!'

Distrust it or not, it was the answer to her prayers, and when Max appeared at the kitchen door, dripping wet again, she even managed to smile.

'Wow,' she said. 'I can't believe you've done this.'

'My pleasure. Do you have a laundry? Can Duncan and I have access?'

'To our laundry?' He was dripping wetly onto the linoleum. 'Do you both want to strip off?'

'I don't have any more clothes,' he told her. 'Donald's waterproofs weren't quite as waterproof as I might have liked. But we now have a clothes dryer.'

'A clothes dryer.' What was he talking about?

'I know. I'm brilliant,' he told her, looking smug. 'A little applause wouldn't go astray.'

'Where did you get a dryer?'

'Mrs Aston and Mr Aston paid for their daughter Emma to install central heating just last week,' he said, and his voice changed.

'Those nappies were too much, I said to Ern, I said. They'll be the death of her, with those twins, and young Jason's only just out of nappies and none too reliable. We didn't have any money when we had kiddies but we have now, what with superannuation and all, so the least we can do is pay for central heating. So we did, and now…what does my Em want with a great hulking tumble-dryer when there's a whole new airing cupboard that can take three times as many nappies? You're very welcome to it.'

Max's accent might be French, but he had Mrs Aston's voice down to a T. Pippa stared—and then she giggled.

'You bought us Emma's tumble-dryer.'

'Applause?'

She smiled and even raised her hands to clap—but then her smile died and her hands dropped. 'Max, this is crazy. We really can't accept.'

'My clothes go in first,' he said. 'That's the price I'm demanding. Oh, and I need something to keep me decent while they dry. Can you find me something?'

She gave up. 'I…sure.'

'Two minutes,' he said. 'Me and Dunc are hauling this thing into your laundry and then I want another hot shower. I'll throw my clothes out; you put them in your brand new tumble-dryer and Bob's your uncle.'

'Bob?'

He frowned, intent. 'Bob's your uncle? I don't have that right?'

'It's not a French idiom.'

'I'm not French.'

'You're from Alp d'Estella?'

'Let's leave discussion of nationalities until I'm dry. I only brought one change of clothes and now everything's wet. Can you find me something dry to wear in two minutes?'

It was more than two minutes. Duncan helped Max cart in the dryer, but as Max disappeared towards the shower Duncan headed for the kitchen and a gossip.

'Who is he?' he wanted to know.

'He's a relation of Gina's from overseas,' she told Duncan. 'Gina never heard a word from that side of the family and they surely didn't help when Gina and Donald were killed. If he's being generous now then maybe it's a guilty conscience.'

'You didn't tell Mr Stubbins that Max might be a prince,' Marc whispered as Duncan finally departed with as much information as she was prepared to give.

'Rain or no rain, if I said that we'd have every busybody in the district wanting to visit.' Pippa lifted a packet of crumpets from the table and carried it reverently to the toaster. 'And I'm not feeling like sharing. There's crumpets and there's butter and honey and I'm thinking I'm having first crumpet.'

'Max says there's fish and chips coming.'

'I have crumpets right here,' she said reverently. 'Food now— or food later? There's no choice.'

'Don't you want fish and chips?'

'You think I can't fit both in? Watch.'

'Don't you have to find Max some clothes?' Marc said, starting to sound worried.

'Yes,' Pippa said, popping four crumpets into their over-sized toaster. 'But crumpets first.' She handed plates to Sophie, butter to Claire and a knife to Marc. 'Let's get our priorities straight.' She chuckled, but she didn't say out loud her next thought. Which was that she had a hunk of gorgeous near-to-royalty naked in her bathroom right now—but what she wanted first was a crumpet.

Priorities.

A crumpet dripping with butter and honey and the arrival of fish and chips later, her conscience gave a sharp prod. She did a quick search for something Max could wear, but came up with nothing. She'd kept Donald's waterproofs because the oversized garments were excellent for milking, but the rest of his clothes had gone to welfare long since. She hesitated, then grabbed a pair of her oversized gym pants—and a blanket.

The bathroom door was open a crack.

'Mr de Gautier?'

'It's Max if you have clothes,' a voice growled. 'If not go away.'

'I sort of have clothes.'

'What do you mean sort of?'

'They might be a bit small.'

A hand came out, attached to a brawny arm. It looked a work hand, she thought, distracted. These weren't the soft, smooth fingers of a man unused to manual work. She thought back to the deft way Max had caught and loaded the wood. Royalty? Surely not. She'd seen bricklayers catch and stack like that, with maximum efficiency.

Who was he? What was he?

She stared for a moment too long and his fingers beckoned imperatively. She gasped, put the clothes in his hand and the fingers retreated.

There was a moment's silence. Then…

'These aren't just too small,' he growled. 'These are ridiculous.'

'It's all I have. That's why I brought the blanket.'

'The waterproofs?'

'Belonged to Donald. Donald's dead. We gave the rest of his stuff to charity.'

'I need charity now.'

'We have a tumble-dryer,' she told him. 'Thanks to you. If you hand out your clothes I'll put them in.'

'And I'll sit in here until they dry?'

'If you're worried about your dignity.' He definitely couldn't be royalty, she thought, suppressing a smile. The idea was preposterous.

'You have the fire going?'

'It's already putting out heat. And the fish and chips have just arrived.' She gave a sigh of pure heaven. 'There's two pieces of whiting each, and more chips than we can possibly eat. Would you like me to bring you some?'

'It's cold in here.'

'Then you have my gym pant bottoms and a blanket. Come on out.'

'Avert your eyes.'

'Shall I tell Claire and Sophie and Marc to avert their eyes as well?'

There was a moment's baffled silence. Then: 'Never mind.' There was a moment's pause while he obviously tugged on her gym pants and then the door opened.

Whoa.

Well-brought-up young ladies didn't stare, but there were moments in a woman's life when it was far too hard to be well brought up. Pippa not only stared—she gaped.

He looked like a body builder, she thought. He was tanned and muscled and rippling in all the right places. He was wearing her pants and they were as stretched on him as they were loose on her. Which was pretty much stretched. His chest was bare.

He should look ridiculous.

He looked stunning.

'You can't be a prince,' she said before she could stop herself and the corners of his mouth turned down in an expression of distaste.

'I'm not.' The rebuttal was hard and sharp and it left no room for argument.

'What are you, then?'

He didn't reply. He was carrying his bundle of wet clothes in one hand and the blanket in the other. He was meant to put the blanket round his shoulders, she thought. He wasn't supposed to be bare from the waist up.

He was bare from the waist up and it left her discomforted.

She was so discomforted she could scarcely breathe.

'What do you mean, what am I?' he demanded at last. 'You mean like in, "Are you an encyclopaedia salesman?"?'

'You're not an encyclopaedia salesman.'

'I'm a builder.'

'A builder.' The thought took her aback. 'How can you be a builder?'

He sighed. 'The same way you get to be an encyclopaedia salesman, I imagine. You find someone who's a builder and you say, "Please, sir, can you teach me what you know about building?"'

'That's what you did.'

'Yes.'

'What do you build?'

'Buildings. Did you say the fish and chips have arrived?'

'They're in the kitchen,' she said with another long look at his bare chest.

'Will you stop it?'

'Stop what?'

'Staring at my chest. Men aren't supposed to look at women's chests. I'd appreciate it if you didn't look at mine.'

'It's a very nice chest.'

Whoops.

She'd been out of circulation for too long, she thought in the ensuing silence. Maybe complimenting a man on his chest wasn't something nicely brought-up women did. He was staring at her as if he'd never experienced such a thing. 'Sorry,' she managed at last. 'Don't look at me like I'm a porriwiggle. I shouldn't have said that.'

'It was a very nice compliment,' he said cautiously. 'What's a porriwiggle?'

'A tadpole and it's not a compliment.' She hesitated and then thought maybe it was. But it was also the truth. 'Anyway, it's not what I should be saying. I should be saying thank you for the food.'

'Why are you destitute?' He smiled. 'Tadpoles don't have money?'

She tugged the door open to the rest of the house, trying frantically to pull herself back into line. 'We're not destitute,' she managed. 'Just momentarily tight, and if we don't hurry there'll be no chips left.'

'I can always buy more.'

'Then you'll get wet all over again. That's the very last garment in this house that you might just possibly almost fit into, so let's stop playing in the rain and go eat.'

He sat by the fire in Pippa's gym pants, eating fish and chips, drinking hot chocolate, staying silent while the life of the farm went on around him.

It was almost as if Pippa didn't know where to start with the questions, he thought, and that was okay as he was having trouble with the answers. Any minute now he'd have to tell them why he was here, but for now it just seemed too hard.

Pippa had taken one look at the meat and the pile of vegetables he'd brought and said, 'Pies.' So now a concoction on the stove was already smelling fantastic. Meanwhile she was rolling pastry and Sophie and Claire were helping.

Marc was hanging wet clothes round the kitchen, on the backs of chairs, over something the kids called a clothes horse, over every available surface.

'You can't hang that over me,' Max said as Marc approached him with a damp windcheater and Marc smiled shyly but proceeded to hang it over the arm of his chair.

'The fire's hot. Pippa says the clothes dryer costs money to run.'

'I'll pay,' Max growled and Pippa looked up from her pastry-making and grimaced.

'That's enough. You've been very generous but there are limits. We're very grateful for the dryer and we will use it, but only when we must.'

He stared at her, bemused. She had a streak of flour across her face. The girls were making plaits of pastry to put on the pies. They were surrounded by a sea of flour and she didn't seem to mind. Had he ever met a woman who worried how much it cost to dry clothes? Had he ever met a woman who looked like she did and was just...unaware?

She was knocking him sideways, he thought, dazed. Which was dumb. He'd had girlfriends in his life—of course he had. He was thirty-five. He'd grown pretty damned selective over the years, and the last woman he'd dated had almost rated a ring. Not quite though. She'd been maybe a bit too interested in the royal connection.

So what was he thinking? He hated the royal connection, so any attraction to Pippa would be disastrous. It was only this weird domesticity that was making him feel like this, he decided. Here were echoes of his childhood at his grandparents' farm. Time out from royalty. Family...

A boy who looked like Thiérry. Cute-as-a-button twins. A snoring old dog.

Pippa.

Pippa had flour on her nose. He had the weirdest desire to kiss…

'Will you stay for dinner?' Marc asked, and he thought no, he needed to say what needed to be said and go. Fast. But he just wanted to…

He bit back his stupid wants. What was he thinking? Launching himself across the kitchen past kids and dog and kissing her? You're losing your mind, boyo.

'I… Pippa, I need to talk to you.'

But she was focused on pies. 'These are ready to put together as soon as I come in from the dairy.' She wiped her hands on her windcheater and smiled ruefully at her floury fingerprints. 'What a mess. No matter. The cows won't mind. But they'll be waiting. I need to start milking.'

'I'll bring the cows in for you,' Marc said, but Pippa shook her head.

'I'll do them myself. Marc, can you look after the girls?' Then she turned to Max, worry behind her eyes. 'I need to go,' she said. 'I assume you'll be leaving as soon as your clothes dry? I… I'll leave Dolores here.'

She was torn, he thought. She needed to milk, but she didn't want to leave the children alone with him. And she couldn't kick him out until his clothes dried. He looked down at Dolores, who was sleeping off one steak and dreaming of another.

'She's a great watchdog.'

Pippa flushed. 'I didn't mean…'

'I know you didn't,' he said gently. 'Do you always milk alone?'

'Marc helps me a bit. We have a place in the shed where the girls can play and I can watch them. But Marc's just got over bronchitis and I don't want him wet again.'

'I can help,' Marc protested, but Pippa shook her head.

'I know you can but I don't want you to. I want you and the girls to stay dry.'

'Are they safe here alone?' Max asked, and then as he saw Marc's look of indignation he thought maybe it was an inappropriate question.

'Marc's more than capable,' Pippa said, hurriedly before Marc could protest. 'He's had to be. But I do have an intercom. I listen in and Marc calls me if there's a problem.'

'There's never a problem,' Marc said stolidly and Max smiled at him. The more he saw of this kid, the more he liked him.

'How long does milking take?'

'About three hours,' Pippa said and Max blinked.

'How many cows?'

'A hundred and twenty.'

'I thought your vats were contaminated.'

'Cows dry out. If you let cows dry off for a week, then there's no more milk until next calving. Which is in six months.'

'So you milk every night and throw the milk away?'

'Twice a day,' Marc corrected him, and turned his big brown eyes straight on Max. 'It's much faster than three hours with two people working,' he said, innocently. 'And these pies will be yummy. We'll have tea much earlier if you help.'

'He's not invited for tea,' Pippa said.

'Yes, he is,' Marc said. 'If he helps you milk.'

'He won't know how to milk.'

'Excuse me,' Max said faintly. 'I can milk.'

They both looked at him as if he'd sprouted wings.

'Cows?' Marc queried and Max grinned.

'Cows.'

'But you're a prince.'

'I'm not a prince. My grandparents had a farm.'

'Hey, Pippa,' breathed Marc. 'He really can milk cows.' He turned back to Max. 'You can stay the night and help Pippa again in the morning. The morning milking's really cold.'

'Hey,' said Pippa.

'He can have Mum and Dad's bedroom. No one else uses it.'

'Who's the adult in this family?' Pippa asked, sounding desperate. 'I haven't invited him to stay.'

'Why can't he stay?' Marc sounded astonished.

Pippa blinked, obviously searching for an answer. 'What if I don't like him?'

'What's not to like?' Marc demanded and Max's chest puffed

out a little. 'I know he looks dumb in your pants…' his chest subsided '…but he's bought us all this stuff. I bet he's rich.'

Rich is better than nothing, he guessed.

'I won't stay if Pippa doesn't want me,' he offered.

'She does want you,' Marc said.

'Pippa gets lonely,' Sophie added, distracted momentarily from her pastry. 'Claire and me have got friends at kindergarten and Marc has friends at school. Not now though 'cos school's closed for winter holidays. But no one talks to Pippa.'

'Sophie…' Pippa said helplessly and spread her hands as if she didn't know where to go from here. 'That's not true.'

'It is,' Marc said stolidly. 'No one likes us 'cos you won't sell the farm.'

'I don't want Max to…' She bit her lip and fell silent. Max looked at her for a long minute. She really was battling the odds, he thought. But then she tilted her chin and steadied.

It'd take a lot to get this woman off course.

'I will help with the milking,' he told her gently. 'And if you don't mind, I would like to stay for dinner. I need to talk to you about the children.'

Pippa's face had been wary. Suddenly now though he saw the edges of fear. 'No.'

'No?'

Her chin jutted just a little higher. 'Alice wasn't proud of her royal heritage,' she told him. 'She said she fled all the way to Australia to get away from it and she was never going back. She said it was utterly corrupt, so if that's why you're here we don't want anything to do with it.'

'You don't think you might be jumping to conclusions?'

'Maybe I am. But you haven't come all this way to buy fish and chips. You want something.'

'Maybe I do.'

'Then tell me now.'

'I'd rather do that when we're alone.'

'No. I don't keep things from the kids and they don't keep things from me. I'm their godmother, their guardian and their friend, and I want to keep it that way.'

She met his look, their gaze holding. She didn't look as if she'd budge.

Why not say it? The twins were involved in artwork with leftover pastry. Marc, though, was listening intently. He was only eight years old. Surely decisions should be made for him.

But he glanced at Marc and he saw the same courage and determination that Pippa had. No, he thought. Pippa's right. He wasn't sure what Marc had been through, but his eyes were wiser than his years. Between Marc and Pippa there seemed to be a bond of unbreakable trust.

So he had to say what he'd come to say. To both of them.

'The Crown Prince of Alp d'Estella died last month,' he said. 'Bernard died childless and there's no one left of his line. The succession therefore goes back to Bernard's grandfather and follows the line down. Thus we reach Marc. Marc is heir to the throne. He's the new Crown Prince of Alp d'Estella.'

CHAPTER THREE

EVEN the twins heard that. Or maybe they heard the loaded silence where Pippa stared at Max, appalled, and he tried to figure what she'd say when she finally found her tongue.

In the end it was Marc who spoke first. 'What's a Crown Prince?'

'It's like a king,' Max told him. 'It's a head of a country that's called a principality rather than a kingdom.'

'Is a Crown Prince rich?'

'Very.'

'We're not rich,' Marc said.

'I realise you're not.' Max turned to Pippa. 'But there is money. Bernard was never…scrupulous in his financial dealings, but as Marc is his heir there should have been provisions. There will be now. I expect this may take all sorts of pressures off.'

'What sort of pressures?' Pippa asked

He hesitated again, still unsure. 'Maybe we need to talk away from the children.'

'The girls aren't listening and this is more Marc's business than mine. I need to milk but I guess we need to have this out first.' She perched on the edge of the table and folded her arms. Marc gave her a dubious glance, then did likewise.

Max had come a long way to say this. It had to be said. But first…

'I didn't expect to see the girls,' he said, tentatively. 'Palace sources said that Marc was an only child.'

'He's not. Claire and Sophie were born just before Gina died. Maybe your palace sources didn't keep up.' Pippa put a hand on Marc's shoulder and gave it a squeeze. 'Will we tell him what happened, Marc?'

'Yes,' Marc whispered. 'Cos he's sort of a cousin.'

'So he is.' Pippa's eyes were carefully expressionless. She sighed, seeming to dredge up energy to tell a dreary story.

'Gina was my best friend,' she said. 'Alice was friend to my mum and she practically adopted me when my mother died. So Gina and I were like sisters. I was bridesmaid at Gina's wedding and godmother to Marc. Gina and Donald were very much in love but they battled to keep this farm going. Alice lived here with them, and I was here a lot, too. Anyway, Alice died just before the twins were conceived. The pregnancy was problematic— Gina was ill and the money was tight. For their wedding anniversary I paid for them to have a weekend in a plush hotel in the city and I came here to milk and to look after Marc. They were killed that weekend.'

'I'm sorry.'

'It was a freak accident,' she said sadly. 'A lorry lost its load and a ton of logs crashed onto them. Donald was killed instantly. Gina lived for six more weeks—long enough for the twins to be born— but she never regained consciousness. She never saw her babies.'

There was a moment's pause. He should say something, he thought. What? 'So you stayed,' he asked at last and she sent him a look that said he was stupid to think she could have done anything else.

'Of course I did. Gina and Donald were my friends. Maybe if it had only been the twins we could have thought of…other options. But I love Marc to bits, and now I love the twins as well.'

'I see.' He hesitated but it had to be said—what needed to be said. 'So you've put your life on hold since Gina's death?'

'I've done no such thing,' she retorted, anger flaring.

'There's no other family?'

'Donald was an only child of elderly parents. They predeceased him by many years. There's no one else.'

'But you were a nurse.'

'And now I'm a dairy farmer. I'm milking cows and sharing my life with Marc and Sophie and Claire and Dolores.'

'My sources say you were a highly skilled nurse.'

'I'm getting pretty renowned in cow circles.'

'This isn't helping,' he said, and she stared at him in astonishment.

'It isn't helping what?'

'Me explaining.'

'You're not explaining. You're making me do the explaining.' She took a deep breath. 'I've talked enough. It's your turn. Go on. Explain.'

'These children are Alp d'Estella's new royal family.'

'These children are eight and four. They're Australian kids.'

'They're that as well, but they have an inheritance in Alp d'Estella.'

She stared. 'What exactly have they inherited?'

'The Crown.'

'A crown's not much use. A dairy farm's a lot more help for paying the bills.'

'I don't see many bills getting paid here.'

'There's no need to get personal. What else do they inherit?'

He paused. This was the crunch, he thought, the factor that had had him thinking all the time that all he had to do was lay the facts before her and he'd have her in the palm of his hand.

But now, suddenly, he wasn't so sure. He glanced at Marc and his words echoed again.

'We're not rich,' Marc had said, but it hadn't been spoken with regret. It was a simple fact.

'The Crown means wealth,' Max said, repeating the words he'd rehearsed when he'd thought he'd known how it would be received. 'Huge wealth.'

'Is Alp d'Estella a wealthy country?'

Max shook his head. He felt weird, he decided. He was barechested in Pippa's kitchen, wearing Pippa's gym pants.

Weird.

'The coffers of the Crown have always been separate from the State,' he said, forging on bravely. 'The royal family of Alp d'Estella has always held onto its wealth.'

'While the peasants starved,' Pippa retorted. 'Alice told us.'

'If he's raised well I believe Marc can go about correcting injustices.'

There was a moment's silence. Pippa's grip on Marc's shoulder tightened. 'So…you'd raise him?' she asked at last.

'No!' It was said with such force that it startled them all. 'No,' he repeated, more mildly this time. 'This has nothing to do with me.'

'Why not?' She frowned. 'Come to think of it… I don't understand. Marc and I read the family tree, or as much as we have of it. If it's male succession, then you seem to be it.'

'No.'

'Or Thiérry…your brother.'

'Thiérry died almost twenty years ago.'

She frowned. 'I guess Alice wouldn't have known that when she wrote the family tree. But…he was in line to inherit after Bernard.'

'Yes.'

'Then why aren't you next?'

'Because the parental names on the birth certificate are different.'

'The names on the birth certificate…' She blinked. He stared right at her, giving her a silent message.

Finally he saw the penny drop.

'Oh,' she said.

'Can we talk about this later?' he asked.

But Pippa seemed too shocked to continue. She blinked a couple more times, then crossed to the back door.

'I have to milk.' She faltered. 'I… If you're here when I get back we'll discuss this then. I'm sorry, but I need to think this through. Look after Max, kids. I just…need time.'

'If there are any questions…'

'Not yet.'

She left. Max was left with Marc and the twins. And Dolores. They were all gazing at him with reproach. Accusing.

'You've made Pippa sad,' Sophie said.

'I haven't,' he said, flummoxed.

'She always goes outside when she's sad,' said Claire.

'She's gone to milk the cows.'

'Yes, but she's sad,' said Marc. 'Maybe she thinks you'll take us away from her.'

'I won't do that.'

'We won't go with you.'

'I don't blame you,' he said, feeling more at sea than he'd ever felt in his life. 'Kids, I promise I'm not here to do anything you don't like. My family and yours were connected a long time ago and now I'm here I'm really upset to find that you're cold and you've been hungry. I want to help, and I won't do anything Pippa doesn't like.'

'Really?' Marc demanded.

'Really.' He met Marc's gaze head-on. Adult to adult.

'I won't be a prince if Pippa doesn't want me to be one,' Marc said.

'I don't blame you.'

He really was a good kid, he thought. Maybe…just maybe this could work. But Marc would have to be protected. And he couldn't be separated from Pippa and the girls. The thought of taking Marc to a distant castle and leaving him with an unknown nanny died the death it deserved. All or nothing.

'I think your Pippa is a really great aunty,' he told them.

'We're lucky.' Marc's expression was still reproving. 'Pippa's ace.' He thought for a minute, his head tilted to the side. 'Is there a castle?'

'In Alp d'Estella, yes.'

'Does it have dragons?' Claire asked.

'No.'

'I don't like dragons,' Sophie said.

'We don't like Pippa being sad,' Marc said, moving the topic back to something he understood. 'She's gone to milk the cows by herself and she's sad.'

'She shouldn't be sad.'

'She gets sad when she thinks about money,' Claire said in a wise voice. 'Did you make her think about money?'

'No. I—'

'Yes, you did,' Marc said. 'So she'll be sad and she's cold and it's raining.' He stared at Max, challenging, and his message was crystal clear.

'You think I should help?' Max said weakly and received three firm nods.

'Yes.'

'I'd better go, then,' he said.

'Don't tell her about dragons,' Sophie said darkly. 'We don't want you to scare her.'

His clothes were still damp. He put them on straight from the tumble-dryer and within minutes they were cold and clammy. He hauled Donald's waterproofs back on—more for the wind factor than anything else as he'd learned by now they made lousy waterproofs.

'Which way's the dairy?' he asked and Marc accompanied him to the edge of the veranda and pointed.

'If you run you won't get too wet,' he said, so Max ran, his oversized gumboots squelching wetly in thick mud.

The dairy was a dilapidated brick structure a couple of hundred yards from the house, with a long line of black and white cows stretching out beside it, sodden and miserable in the rain.

Max walked through a room containing milk vats. The milk wasn't going into the vats, though. It was being rerouted to the drain.

Through the next door was the dairy proper. Pippa was working in a long, narrow pit, with cows lined up on either side.

She had her handkerchief to her eyes as he walked in. She whisked it away the moment she saw him, swiping her sleeve angrily across her eyes and concentrating on washing the next udder.

She'd been crying?

He tried to think of this situation from her point of view. Surely help with the responsibility of raising three kids had to be welcome?

But, he thought with sudden perspicacity, he was related to the children and she wasn't. She loved these kids. Maybe he'd scared her.

Hell, he hadn't meant to.

'I'm here to help,' he told her, and she finished wiping the udder of the nearest cow and started fitting cups.

'Stay back. Cows don't like strangers.'

'They can handle a bit of unease. Let me put on the cups.' He stepped down into the pit before she could protest. 'You bring them in for me. Once they're in a bail they'll hardly notice I'm not you.'

She looked up then, really looked, blatantly astonished. 'You do know how to milk?'

'I don't tell lies, Pippa,' he said gently. 'I've spent time on a dairy farm, yes. And our farm had an outdated herring-bone dairy just like this one.'

Without a word she backed a little, then watched as he washed the next udder and fitted cups. The cow made no protest. Max was wearing familiar waterproofs and in this sort of weather one waterproofed human was much like another.

Satisfied—but still silent—she headed into the yard to bring the next cow in.

This would essentially halve her time spent in the dairy, Max thought. If Pippa had been forced to bring cows in herself, stepping out of the pit and back down time and time again, it'd take well over three hours, morning and night. Six hours of milking in this weather as well as all the other things that had to be done on a farm, plus looking after the children—and now the vats were contaminated and the milk was running down the drain.

What the hell was she doing here?

But he wasn't the first to ask questions. 'So tell me about this royal thing,' she called as the next cow came calmly into the bail. She had a radio on as background noise, so she had to speak loudly. 'What do you mean different parental names? Is that why Alice put a question mark against your name on the family tree?'

'You've seen the family tree?'

'Alice drew me one for us, a long time ago. It's what she remembered and heard from friends back home, but it's sketchy. You're on there. So's Thiérry. But there's a question mark after you. Why?'

'It's a sordid family story.'

'It can't be any more sordid than mine,' she said flatly. 'If it affects Marc, then I need the truth.'

He shrugged. He'd hated saying it, but then it had achieved what it was meant to achieve. 'My mother was married to Edouard, the Crown Prince Etienne's grandson. Bernard's cousin. She and my father had Thiérry. Then my mother had an affair. She was still married when I was born but my father doesn't appear on the birth certificate.'

There was a moment's silence while she thought that through. Then: 'So you can't inherit?'

'No.'

'But you've had a lot to do with royalty?'

'No. My mother had nothing to do with Bernard or his father. We've been in France since I was a baby.'

'You speak great English.'

'My Grandma on my mother's side is English. She drummed English into me from the time I was a tot, refusing to let me grow into what she called a little French Ruffian. She'd be delighted you noticed!'

'Right.' She nodded, more to herself than to him. She hauled her handkerchief from her pocket and gave her nose a surreptitious blow. Then she put her shoulders back, as if she was giving herself courage. She ushered another cow forward, and then, astonishingly, she started to sing.

An old pop song was playing on the radio. Max recognised it from years ago. Many years ago. His grandmother had liked this song. 'Tell Laura I Love Her' was corn at its corniest, but Pippa was suddenly singing as loud as she could, at full pathos, relishing every inch of tragedy.

The cows didn't blink.

He did. He straightened and stared. Pippa was a wet, muddy, bedraggled figure in a sea of mud and cows. Five minutes ago she'd been crying. He was sure she'd been crying.

She was singing as if the world were at her feet.

He went back to cleaning, putting on cups, taking cups off. Listening.

'Tell Laura' was replaced by 'The Last Waltz' and she didn't do a bad rendition of that either. Then there was Olivia Newton-John's 'I Am Woman' and she almost brought the house down. He found himself grinning and humming—but a lot more quietly than Pippa.

'You don't sing?' she demanded as she sang the last note and gave her next cow an affectionate thump on the rump.

'Um…no.'

'Not even in the shower?'

'I'm admitting nothing.'

She chuckled. 'That means you do. Why don't you sing along?'

'I'm enjoying listening to you.'

'So sing with me next time.' But the next song was one neither of them knew, which was clearly unsatisfactory.

'I'll write to their marketing manager,' she said darkly. 'Putting on newfangled songs I don't know the words of is bad box office.'

'So what do you have to sing about?' he asked into the lull.

'I can't find anything to sing about with this song.'

He glanced at the source of the music—a battered radio sitting at the end of the bales. 'You want me to change the channel?'

'There speaks a channel surfer,' she said. 'Men! They spend their lives looking for something better and miss out on the good stuff.'

'Good stuff like "I Am Woman"?'

'Exactly.'

'So what's put you off men…exactly?'

'Life,' she said theatrically and gave an even more theatrical sigh. 'Plus the fact that no one finds my fashion sense sexy.'

Fashion? He could hardly see her. She was a diminutive figure in waterproofs that were far too big for her. Her boots were caked in mud and there was a fair bit of dung attached as well. She was a shapeless, soggy mass, but she was patting the cow before her with real affection, waiting for the next song to start before launching herself into her own personal theatrical performance.

Was she sexy? Maybe not but here it was again, a stirring of something that was definitely not unsexy interest.

Which was crazy, he told himself again, even more severely than the last time he'd told himself. He'd come here for one reason and one reason only. He expected to put Marc on the plane to Alp d'Estella—with or without attachments—and then get the hell out of this mess. He'd thought this through. He could fit the requirements of the regency in with his current work. He'd install Charles Mevaille as administrator. Charles was more competent than he'd ever be. Sure there'd be times when he needed to intervene personally, but for the most part he could get himself back to the life that he loved.

Did he love his life?

Whoa. What was he thinking? He surely loved his life better than a life of being in the royal goldfish bowl—and he liked his life better than the one this woman was leading.

But she sang. She sang straight after she cried.

So she was better at putting on a cheerful face than he was. The singing must be a part of that, he realised. It was a tool to force herself away from depression.

Why was she here?

He washed the udder of a gently steaming cow, and attached the cups with skills he'd learned as a kid. Despite her singing, Pippa hadn't relaxed completely. She was watching him, he knew, uncertain yet that she could trust him with cows that were her livelihood.

What had she been facing if he hadn't turned up this afternoon? What would they have eaten? Maybe Pippa would have figured some way to feed them. She looked like a figuring type of woman.

But the house had been freezing, and she hadn't figured out a way to stop that. Surely this farm wasn't a long-term proposition?

It couldn't be, and that must make a proposition of another life welcome. But he wasn't sure. She'd obviously been told enough of Alp d'Estella's royal family to react with disgust.

That wasn't surprising. Alice—Gianetta's mother—had fled to Australia for much the same reasons as his own mother had fled to France. Alice had done it much more successfully though, living her life in relative obscurity.

'Excuse me, but Peculiar's cups need taking off,' Pippa called, hauling him back to the here and now. He'd been wiping teats and putting on cups without paying attention to the end of the queue. But…

'Peculiar?'

'The lady with the white nose and the empty teats at the end of the line. She was first in and now she's ready to leave.'

'You call a cow Peculiar?'

'You want to know why?'

'Yes.' He removed Peculiar's cups and released her from her bail. She didn't go.

'See,' Pippa said.

'If I had the choice I wouldn't want to head out into the dark and stormy night either.'

'She never wants to go outside. And when she's out she doesn't want to come in. The other cows look at her sideways.'

'So you gave her a nice reassuring name like Peculiar.'

'I could have called her Psycho but I didn't.'

He gave the cow a slap on the rump. 'Out.'

Peculiar retaliated by kicking straight back at him. But Max had spent years of his life in a dairy and he was fast. He sidestepped smartly, just out of range of the slashing hooves.

'Neatly done,' Pippa said. 'But see? Psycho. I always milk her first and get her out of the way.'

'You could have called her Psycho then.' Peculiar was ambling out now, content that there was no more opportunity to wreak havoc. 'Peculiar gives warm connotations of a mildly eccentric aunt.'

'I'm a nice person. I'm giving her leeway to reform.'

He stared out at her through the rain. Pippa was nice? She definitely was, he thought. Nice, and very, very different.

'What the hell are you doing on a dairy farm?' he demanded.

'Same as you. Milking cows.'

'But you're a nurse.'

'That was my first job. I have better things to do with my life now.'

'Since Gina and Donald were killed.'

'What do you think? Should I say, Ooh, my career in nursing is far more important than taking care of my best friend's orphaned children? Don't stop now, Mr de Gautier. Big-bum's waiting for her cups.'

'Big-bum.'

'The next cow,' she retorted. 'Do what I do for a bit, Mr de Gautier. Do what comes next and don't look further.'

She turned her back on him, ostensibly to bring in the next cow, but he suspected it was more than that—a ruse to bring the conversation to an abrupt end.

Which suited him. He had enough information to assimilate for the time being.

Marc's voice came back to him. 'This is our Pippa.' It had been a declaration of family.

Would Our Pippa agree to accompany the kids?

Do what comes next and don't look further. He attended to Big-bum. She was indeed…Big-bum?

He shook his head, trying to clear emotions that were strange and unwelcome. He was here to give a message and go. He was not here to learn by heart a hundred and twenty cows' names.

Pippa looked about fourteen, Max thought. And then he thought: She looks frightened.

She ushered in half a dozen more cows and he milked in silence. There were a couple of soppy songs on the radio but she'd stopped singing.

'You're here to take the children to Alp d'Estella,' she said into the stillness and he raised his head and met her challenging look head-on. Not for long though. Her eyes were bright with anger and he was starting to feel…ashamed? Which was crazy. This was a fantastic opportunity he was handing these children. He had no reason to feel ashamed.

'And you,' he admitted. 'If you want to go.'

'When did you arrive in Australia?'

'About nine hours ago.'

'From France?'

'Yes.'

'Then you'll have jet lag,' she whispered, so softly he barely heard. 'You'll not be making sense. We'll leave this discussion for later. Meanwhile turn the radio up, would you? It's not loud enough.'

'You don't want to talk any more?'

'Not now and maybe not ever,' she snapped. 'Our life is here. Meanwhile let's get these ladies milked.'

'You need to think about—'

'I don't need to think about anything,' she snapped. 'I need to sing. Turn the radio up and let me get on with it.'

'Yes, ma'am.' There was nothing left for him to say.

* * *

It took them just under two hours. Pippa saw the last cow amble back down to the paddocks with relief. She closed the gate and turned to fetch the hose but Max swung out of the milking pit and reached the hose before her.

'I'll sluice the dairy,' he told her. 'You go in and get warm.'

'I need to clean the vats.'

'Why? We haven't used them.'

'I have to figure what caused the contamination.'

'Old tubing?'

'Maybe, but I can't afford new so all I can do is scrub.'

If the tubing was corroded no amount of scrubbing would help and from the despair etched behind her eyes he thought she knew it. 'Pippa, don't worry about it tonight,' he said gently. 'You look exhausted.'

'You're the one with jet lag.'

'You're the one who looks like you have jet lag.'

She flushed. 'There's nothing wrong with me that another hot shower won't cure.'

He smiled at that, thinking of how many hot showers had been enjoyed today. 'Lucky you have a decent hot water service.'

'If we ran out of hot water I might be tempted to walk away,' she told him. 'But don't worry. I won't. Regardless of your plans for our family.'

'Pippa…'

'I'm going,' she said and cast him a darkling look. 'I don't have a clue what's going on, so I'll take a shower and leave you to my dairy.'

She left him to it. By the time she reached the door he was already working methodically with the hose, sluicing from highest level to lowest. He knew what he was doing.

Which was more than she did.

She knew so little of this royal bit—only what Alice had told Gina. But: 'We're best out of it,' she'd said. 'Gina needs have nothing to do with them, and neither do I. They're corrupt and they're evil. It's a wonder the country hasn't overthrown them with force. Anyway I refuse to look back. I'll only look forward.'

Alice had died too young, Pippa thought sadly—a lovely,

gracious lady who'd made Pippa's life so much happier since Gina had brought home her 'best friend from school'.

Pippa owed them everything. She and Gina had been so close they were almost sisters. They were both only children of single mothers, but Gina's mother had cared, whereas Pippa's...

'Gina and Alice were my family,' Pippa told herself as she squelched through the mud on her way back to the house. 'And Gina's kids are now my kids. If Max What's-His-Name thinks he can step in and take over...'

She shook herself, literally, and a shower of water sprayed out around her. Dratted men. Men meant trouble and Maxsim de Gautier meant more trouble than most. She knew it.

But right now he was back in the dairy and she'd reached home.

She poked her nose through the back door and warmth met her and the smell of the makings of her pie simmering on the stove and the sound of Sophie and Claire giggling. They were sitting in front of the fireguard playing with their dolls. Dolores had nosed the fireguard aside and was acting as a buffer between twins and fire, soaking up all the heat in the process.

She was a great watchdog, Pippa thought fondly, and then she thought: Max has done this.

But if he thinks he can seduce me...

Wrong word, she thought, suddenly confused. It was a dopey word. It should have been if he thinks he can influence me with money...

The seduce word stayed in her mind, though, refusing to be banished.

Marc had been setting the table—with their best crockery, she noted with astonishment. When he saw Pippa alone in the doorway his face drooped in disappointment.

'He's gone.'

'He's coming after me. He's sluicing the dairy.'

The droop turned into a grin. He laid cutlery at the head of the table—a position they never used. 'Have a shower and put something pretty on,' he told her.

'I don't have something pretty.'

'Yes, you do. The stuff you wear to church.'

'The pink cardigan,' Sophie volunteered.

'It's a bit old,' Claire added. 'But it's still pretty.'

But he's dangerous, she thought.

But she didn't say it. She couldn't. She was being ridiculous.

She was the children's legal guardian. Max had no rights at all where they were concerned.

And he had no right to make her feel that he was…dangerous…where she was concerned.

She showered, and in deference to the kids' decree she donned her church clothes—a neat black skirt and a pretty pink twin-set. It was a bit priggish, she thought, staring into the mirror, but it was the best she had, and she wasn't out to impress Max.

But she did shampoo her hair and blow-dry her curls, brushing until they shone. She did apply just a little powder and lipstick. But that was all.

She turned from her reflection with a rueful grimace. Once upon a time she and Gina had spent hour upon giggly hour getting ready for special evenings. Now Gina was dead and the only cosmetics Pippa possessed were a compact for a shiny nose and a worn lipstick. And the only good outfit she had was her church gear.

Enough. She stuck her tongue out at her reflection. She headed back to the kitchen, but paused before she entered. There was the sound of kids giggling and Max's deep voice talking to them.

On impulse she deviated to the office.

The office was a bit of a misnomer. It was a tiny space enclosed at the end of the veranda. Pippa stored the farm paperwork here, and she had an ancient computer with dial-up internet connection—as long as the phone lines weren't down. They weren't. She typed in Alp d'Estella and found out what it had to say.

Of the group of four alpine nations—Alp Quattro—in southern Europe, Alp d'Estella is the largest. The four countries depend heavily on tourists; and indeed each country has stunning scenery. Alp d'Estella is known throughout the world for its magnificent shoe trade. Alp d'Estella's skilled tradesmen supply exquisitely made handmade shoes to the catwalks of London, Paris, New York and Rome.

Politically, however, there is trouble in paradise. Each of the Alp Quattro countries is a Principality and their constitutions leave absolute power in the hands of the Crown Prince. Alp d'Azuri, a neighbouring country, has with the help of the current Crown Prince, moved to revoke these powers and is now seen as politically stable. Alp d'Estella, however, is a country in crisis.

The death of the Crown Prince a month ago with no clear successor has left the country more corrupt than when the Prince was alive. Prince Bernard led a puppet government which, if no one claims the throne, will become the de-facto government. Poverty is widespread, as is corruption. The nation's only industries are being taxed to the hilt and are now threatened with bankruptcy. The succession must be sorted, and sorted quickly, in order to restore order.

This was why Max was here. To organise the succession. To an eight-year-old.

What did Marc know about running a country?

Nothing. It was ridiculous. But there was no time to discover more.

She took a deep breath, disconnected and went to tell Max how ridiculous it was.

CHAPTER FOUR

PIPPA couldn't tell Max anything for a while, for the children had decreed tonight a party.

Pippa could hardly believe the transformation. They'd all just recovered from world's worst cold virus, with Marc sickest of all. The last few weeks had been dank and miserable. Cold seemed to have seeped into their bones, but now she couldn't hear so much as a residual cough. With the warmth and with the wonderful food—and maybe with the excitement of Max's visit?—they'd found a new lease of life. The twins had put on their best dresses. They'd tied a huge red bow around Dolores' neck—she looked very festive fast asleep by the stove. And, from a sad, coughing little boy, Marc was transformed into master of ceremonies, bossing everyone.

'Give Mr de Gautier red lemonade,' he ordered Pippa when they sat down to eat, and when Pippa didn't move fast enough he sighed and started pouring himself.

'He's bought wine,' Pippa said mildly, but the children stared at her as if she had to be joking—wine when there was red lemonade?—and Max accepted his red lemonade with every semblance of pleasure and raised a glass in crimson toast.

'You see what it's like?' Pippa demanded, smiling and raising her glass in turn. 'I try to be in charge…'

'Pippa's no good at being bossy,' Marc told Max, and Max grinned.

'She was pretty non-bossy in the dairy. I'm thinking she's more an opera singer than a dairy maid.'

The operatic singer blushed crimson. 'There's no need…'

'Now, don't defend yourself,' he said, ladling pie onto the twins' plates. 'There's no need. It was truly marvellous singing. It's a wonder the milk didn't turn to curds and whey all by itself.'

'You…'

'What?'

She stared at him. He kept right on smiling and she kept right on staring. The table stilled around them.

'Would you like some pie?' he asked gently and she gasped and reached for the pie dish with her bare hands. Which was dumb. There was a dish cloth lying ready but she hadn't used it. The pie dish was very hot. She yelped.

He was up in a flash, tugging her chair back. Propelling her to the sink.

'I'm fine,' she managed, but he had her hands under the tap and it was already running cold.

'I hardly touched it.'

'You yelped.' His hands were holding hers under the water, brooking no opposition.

'I did not yelp.'

'You did so,' Marc volunteered from behind them. 'Are you burned?'

'Do you need a bandage?' Claire demanded, then slipped off her chair and headed for the bathroom without waiting for a response. 'You always need a bandage,' she said wisely.

'I hardly touched it,' she said again, and Max lifted her fingers from the water and inspected them one by one. There was a faint red line on one hand, following the curve of her fingers.

'Ouch?' he said gently and he smiled.

There was that smile. Only it changed every time he used it, she thought. He was like a chameleon, fitting to her moods. Using his smile to make her insides do strange things. She looked up at him, helpless, and Sophie sighed dramatically in the face of adult stupidity and handed her the dishcloth.

'Dry your hands,' she said and edged Max away. 'We don't need bandages,' she called to her twin. 'There's no blood. You'll be all right, won't you?' she told Pippa. 'There's chocolate ice cream for dessert.'

'You guys are amazing,' Max said. 'You take it in turns to play boss.'

'It works for us.' Pippa tugged her hands away—which took some doing—and returned to her place at the table with what she hoped was a semblance of dignity. 'Everything's fine.'

But everything wasn't fine. Everything was…odd. Max was still smiling as he ladled her pie without being asked.

Her insides felt funny.

It was hunger, she told herself.

She knew it was no such thing.

The rest of dinner passed uneventfully, which was just as well for Pippa's state of mind. She ate in silence. The children chattered to Max, excited by the food, the festive occasion and the fact that this big stranger seemed interested in everything they said. He seemed really nice, she thought, but she tried to keep her attention solidly on food.

'I need to put the kids to bed,' she said when the last of the chocolate ice cream had been demolished. 'Don't wash up until I get back.'

'I'm helping Max wash up,' Marc said and Pippa practically gaped.

'You're offering?'

'If Max can do dishes then I can.'

She gazed at him, doubtfully—this little boy who was growing to be a man.

She knew nothing of raising boys, she thought. She knew nothing of…men. She had nothing to do with them. There was not a single inch of room in her life for anything approaching romance.

Romance? Where had that thought come from?

From right here, she told herself as she ordered the twins to bed. For some dumb reason she was really attracted to Max.

Well, any woman would be, she told herself. It's not such a stupid idea. He's connected to royalty, he has a yummy accent and he's drop-dead gorgeous.

So you're not dumb thinking he's attractive. You're just dumb thinking anything could come of it.

Dumb or not, she read the twins a really long book and tucked them in with extra cuddles. She called Marc and did the same for him. When she finally finished, Max was in the living room, ensconced in an armchair by the fire, with Dolores draped over his feet.

Pippa had hardly been in this room since summer. It was cold and unwelcoming and slightly damp. Now however the fire had been roaring in the firestove for hours. Max was cooking crumpets on a toasting fork. He'd loaded a side-table with plates and butter and three types of jam. The whole scene was so domestic it made Pippa blink.

'Haven't we just had dinner?'

'Yes, but I saw the toasting fork and I need to try it. And now I'm feeling like crumpets, too.'

The fire was blazing. 'How much wood are you using?' she said before she thought about it and Max cast her a look of soulful reproach.

'There's more where it came from and the least you can do is make a guest feel warm.'

'You're no guest.' She was feeling desperate and desperate times called for desperate measures. Or bluntness at least. 'You're here to take Marc.'

'Don't dramatise. You know I can't do that. You're Marc's guardian. Well done?'

She blinked. 'Sorry?'

'How do you like your crumpet?' he asked patiently. 'I'm getting good at this. The first crumpets ended up in the fire—this toasting fork has no holding power. But the last one I made was excellent. You can have this one. Do you like it slightly singed or charcoal-black?'

'We'll be out of wood again by the end of the week, and I'm not letting you buy more.'

'I'm hoping you'll be in Alp d'Estella by the end of the week.'

Pippa took a deep breath. Things were happening way too fast.

'We're not going to Alp d'Estella. You can't have Marc.'

'He has a birthright,' Max said, flipping his crumpet.

'Maybe he has, but it's here.' She closed her eyes. The effort she'd been making since Max had arrived slipped a little. Her vocals in the dairy had been a last-ditch attempt to find control and it hadn't worked.

She felt so tired she wanted to sleep for a month.

'Pippa, this is impossible,' Max said, laying his crumpet down, rising and pushing her into the chair he'd just vacated. 'Tell me why you're doing this?'

'Doing…what?'

'Trying to keep this farm going against impossible odds.'

'It's all the children have,' she whispered. 'It's all I have.'

'I don't understand.' He shifted the sleeping Dolores sideways. Dolores didn't so much as open an eye. He hauled another chair up beside her and sat down. 'I need background.'

'It's none—'

'It is my business,' he said gently. 'It seems to me that I'm the only relation these kids have. Now that doesn't give me any rights,' he said hurriedly as he saw alarm flit across her face. 'But it does make me concerned, succession to the throne or not. Tell me about you. About this whole family.'

She hesitated. She shouldn't tell him. What good would it do? But he was looking at her with eyes that said he was trying to understand, that he might even want to help. The sensation was so novel that she was suddenly close to tears.

She fought them back. No way was she crying in front of him.

'Why is the farm so poor?' he asked.

'I told you,' she said, rattled. 'The vats are contaminated.'

'You were poor before that.'

'It's not a wealthy farm.'

'And?'

'And Gina and Donald didn't have insurance. They couldn't afford it. Then the medical costs for Gina and the twins were exorbitant, as was paying someone to keep this place going until I could cope. I'm paying that off still.'

'Is the farm freehold?'

'There are still debts.'

'But a sizeable chunk is paid for?'

'Yes.'

'According to the ladies in the Tanbarook supermarket you could sell it tomorrow.'

'I could,' she said and bit her lip. 'Actually I have two buyers. The developers who want to use it as a road, or the Land for Wildlife Foundation. There's a project going to make a wilderness corridor from the coast to the mountains north of here, and this place would be an important link.' She managed a smile. 'They'd pay less but if it was up to me I'd sell the land to them.' Her smile faded. 'But of course it's not up to me.'

'Why not?' He frowned. 'You could sell, to whoever you choose to sell to, and you could take another nursing job.' Then as she started to protest he placed his finger on her lips. It was a weird gesture of intimacy that felt strangely right for here. For now. 'Hush,' he told her. 'I'm not stupid. I accept you won't leave the children. But I'd assume you could get a reasonable income from nursing, and the farm would bring in something. That must mean you could have a life where you'd at least be warm and well fed.'

'The kids' inheritance is the farm. That's all they have.'

'I disagree. They have you. An inheritance isn't worth starving for.'

'You don't think it's important?'

'Not that much.'

'Then why are you going to this trouble to make sure Marc inherits this principality?'

He hesitated. Then he spread his hands, as if deciding to tell all. 'There are lives at stake.'

She stared. 'That sounds ridiculous.'

'It's true.'

'Really?'

'Really.'

'Why?'

'If there's no Crown Prince then the country reverts to political rule, which at the moment would practically be a dictatorship. That's why you haven't heard of Marc's inheritance before this. The politicians want nothing more than for the royal succession to die and for them to be in sole charge. The local farmers are being bled dry with taxes as it is. If it gets worse…well, I'm not overstating it when I say there will be starvation.'

'But that's…that's crazy. Marc can't have anything to do with that.'

'He doesn't need to. He simply needs to be allowed to take on the title. The rest can be managed around him.' He hesitated, and then forged on. 'Because my mother was still married to Edouard when I was born and because I was half-brother to Thiérry, I can accept the role of Prince Regent. That means until Marc is twenty-one, I can make decisions for him. We can get the country back on track.'

'But…' she shook her head '…this is nonsense. How can I possibly expose Marc to something so weird?'

'It's not so weird,' he said and smiled. 'It's lovely. You could come for a holiday and see. When did you last have a holiday?'

She stared at him blankly.

His smile faded. 'When, Pippa?'

'I…when I was nursing I'd come here sometimes and help.'

'Have you ever taken the children on a holiday?'

'No, but—'

'Alp d'Estella's in the middle of summer right now,' he said persuasively. 'The castle's great.'

'Claire says it'll have dragons.'

'Dragons?'

'All castles have dragons,' she said, distracted. 'Or at least something scary.' She shook her head as if trying to clear fog. 'You want Marc to be Crown Prince? He's far too young to be anything of the kind.'

'It's Crown Prince in name only. Until he's of age the responsibility is mine.' He hesitated. 'Pippa, I know Alice didn't trust the royal family, but the old line is dead. Marc represents the new line. A new hope for the future.'

She took a deep breath. 'It sounds nonsensical,' she whispered. 'How can I possibly trust you?'

'You don't need to trust me,' Max said, steadily, as if he wasn't offended and had in fact anticipated her qualms. 'I've set my credentials before your Minister of International Affairs and he'll vouch for my integrity. My mother also knows your country-woman, Jessica, who married my neighbour, Raoul, Crown Prince of Alp d'Azuri. I believe your women's magazines have written her up, so maybe you've heard of her? Jessie's pregnant and blissfully happy, but she's not so tied up in her own content-ment that she doesn't interest herself in the affairs of her neigh-bours. Both she and her husband have sent their personal assurance that Marc will be safe. They guarantee that if you don't think it's satisfactory then you're free to take Marc and leave. At any time.'

She blinked. She had indeed heard of Jessica, the Australian fashion designer who by all reports was living happily ever after in her fairy-tale palace with her handsome prince. The Princess Jessica had written her an assurance? The whole thing was unbelievable.

There were so many questions. She could only manage a little one. An important one. 'It's warm?'

He smiled. 'It's warm,' he said softly. 'Not only that, we have three swimming pools—a lap pool, an outdoor recreational pool and one indoors and heated for inclement weather. Not that it'll be inclement at this time of the year. It'll be beautiful.'

He was seducing her with sunshine. She had to keep her head.

'You would be able to leave,' he added, gently but definitely, and his big hands came out and covered hers. 'I promise, Pippa. I'm asking that you come for a month. One month. Then you'll know the facts. You'll know what's on offer. You can make up your mind from a position of knowledge.'

'But the cost,' Pippa said weakly. She should pull her hands away but she couldn't make herself do it.

'It's taken care of already.' Then as she looked startled the pressure on her hands intensified. There was no way it should make her feel secure and safe, but stupidly it did. 'Pippa, I know I'm pushing you,' he said. 'But I'm in a hurry. The succession has to be worked out fast. Yes, you have some thinking to do but you can't think without having seen what's on offer. A sensible woman would come.'

'Sometimes I'm not sensible,' she said and she glowered and his smile changed a little, genuine amusement behind his eyes.

'I can see that. But maybe your sensible side will out?'

She stared at him, nonplussed. The lurking twinkle was dangerous, she thought. Really dangerous.

Concentrate on practicalities. 'But there's passports and things…'

'I have friends in high places. I can have passports in twenty-four hours.'

'Twenty-four hours? Are you some kind of magician?'

'Just a man who's determined to have you see what you need to see.'

She was dumbfounded. 'But…the cows,' she whispered at last, and Max grinned as if that was the last quibble out of the way.

'I talked to Bert. He'll be more than happy to take over the milking for now. I gather he did it before? He'll use his dairy and his vats are clean, so he can be paid for the milk. No obligation, he said, and why would there be? He'll even milk Peculiar.'

'You know Bert wants to buy us out. This is making it easier for him.'

'Maybe it is but we're making no promises,' Max said evenly. 'You're just taking time to think. It won't increase the pressure. Regardless of what you decide, these children are eligible for lifetime support from the royal coffers. You'll never be hungry again. I promise.' The grip on her hand strengthened, a warm, strong link that made her feel…wonderful. 'I swear.'

She blinked and blinked again. She would not cry.

This was a fairy tale. She shouldn't let herself be conned. But in truth… In truth she'd fallen from the roof last week and it had scared her witless. Not for herself so much as for the children. She was all they had. If anything happened to her…

She had to think about it.

And warmth…

'Who else will be at the castle?' she managed, trying desperately to focus on practicalities.

'Servants.'

'How many servants?'

'Thirty or more. I'm not sure.'

Her eyes widened. She should pull her hands away, she thought desperately, but she sort of…couldn't.

'Your family?' she whispered. 'Your mother?' She hesitated but she knew absolutely nothing of this man and there was one question that was pretty major waiting to be asked. 'Your wife?'

'My mother's in Paris,' he said evenly. 'And I'm not married. But that's of no importance as I won't be at Alp d'Estella myself. I'll escort you there and then leave.'

She blinked. He'd leave? 'Why?'

'I have no place in Alp d'Estella. It's Marc who inherits. Not me.'

Her hand was withdrawn at that, hauled away before he could react and tucked firmly in the folds of her skirt, as if she was afraid he might try to reclaim it. He couldn't. The fairy tale was dissipating. 'Now, hang on a minute,' she said. 'You're expecting to dump us and run?'

'I wouldn't put it quite like that.' The twinkle faded.

'How would you put it? You've given us all these assurances but if you're not there how can I know they'll be held good?' She frowned. 'Anyway, what does Prince Regent mean?'

'It's a caretaker role. I get to do the paperwork, and make decisions on behalf of the heir to the Crown until he's of age. I can do that from Paris, mostly.'

'But if you're illegitimate—how can you be Regent?'

'There's no one else.'

'I don't understand.'

'I've only just had it explained to me myself,' he said ruefully. 'But it seems the Alp d'Estella constitution—or whatever they call it when it's to do with royal succession—has a stipulation that the regency can be held by someone with blood ties to an heir to the throne. Parent, sibling or half-sibling. I guess it was drawn up in the days when death in childbirth was common, and so was death in battle. An older half-sister may well be all there was to care for the rights of a young prince.'

'But…if your real father isn't royal…'

'That's why I'm here four weeks after Bernard died and not before. I thought I had nothing to do with it. However there are people in Alp d'Estella desperate to see the current regime displaced. They realised the vague constitutional wording—blood ties to *an* heir rather than *the* heir—meant that I could take the regency on. If I don't take it on, the politicians will, and there's no way you could let Marc walk into that.'

'So what do you get out of it?'

'Nothing. But the country is desperate for decent rule.' He hesitated. 'Do you know anything about the Alp countries?'

'Not much.'

'They're four principalities,' he said, sighing, as if this was a tale he'd wearied of telling. 'And they've been degenerate for generations. The princes running them come from a long line of families where indulgence is everything. We now have corrupt politicians who know the only way to advance is to please royalty. The Crown Prince of our nearest neighbour, Alp d'Azuri, has set about changing that. Raoul—your Jessica's husband—has used his sovereign powers to instil a democracy. The change is wonderful. That's where the idea came from that change is possible, but it can't be done unless Marc accepts the Crown.'

'But Marc's too young to decide.'

'It doesn't matter. Once he's installed as Crown Prince, no matter how old he is, measures can be put in place to get the country on an even keel. He can forfeit the Crown later if he wants, but I do need time to get a proper parliament in place.'

'You can do that?'

'From the background, it seems that, yes, I can.'

Pippa sat back in her chair and stared at him. Awed. 'You mean what I agree on, right now, right here, while I'm still thawing from milking, will affect the lives of…'

'Millions. Yes, it will. But don't let me pressure you.'

'You're mad.'

'Yes, but I bought you steak and firewood and I helped you milk. I can't be all bad.'

She shook her head, trying to clear her jumbled thoughts. 'Don't think you can inveigle me into doing stuff. I didn't ask for help.'

'I don't want to inveigle you to do anything.'

'Bully for you.' Pippa was feeling so lost she didn't know where she was. She picked up the toasting fork and absently held the half-cooked crumpet to the flames again. Then she put it down. She couldn't concentrate.

'All I know of this country is from you,' she whispered.

'That's right. But I can give you assurances, and not just from me.'

'But, you see, I'm all the children have,' she said apologetically. 'How can I put them at risk?'

'You won't be putting them at risk.'

'But you won't be there.' She took a deep breath. 'We could come,' she admitted. 'I might even be prepared to take a chance. But only if you were there.'

'I can't.'

'Why not?'

'I have a life. My building—'

'I had a life too once,' she snapped. 'My nursing. I've put my life on hold for these kids. So how important is forming a parliament? You'd put your life on hold for how long for this kingdom of yours?'

'It's a principality.'

'Kingdom—principality—it makes no difference,' she snapped. 'But I won't do this alone. It scares me stupid. I won't let you guilt me into it because the country might starve, and then watch you walk away and leave me to do it alone. You're a de Gautier. Illegitimate or not, you know the reputation of your family. Alice ran for a reason and I'm not as stupid as I look.'

'I never said—'

'You don't have to say,' Pippa said. 'Stupid is as stupid does. You hold this place out to me like a carrot on the end of a stick. Warmth. Castles. Swimming pools. And you…a Prince Regent who looks like you stepped out of a romance movie, telling me I have to agree or the peasants will starve…'

'You don't think you're being just a touch melodramatic?'

'Of course I'm being melodramatic,' she yelled, so loudly that Dolores was forced to raise her head in faint reproach.

'There's no need to yell,' Max said, starting to sound exasperated, but she'd gone too far to draw back now.

'There is. I have no guarantee that you care one bit about this little boy you barely know. Or his sisters. I won't be bludgeoned into taking them to a country I don't know, unless I have some cast-iron guarantees.' She held up each finger in turn. 'One, you agree that we're staying for a month and only a month. We can all leave freely any time after that, and if the children are unhappy then we can leave earlier. Two, you organise that this farm will be cared for while we're away. You seem to have enough money. Three, you agree that Marc is not to be made aware that anyone's welfare depends on him. Four, you stay for the entire month. You leave whatever you do in Paris as you're asking me to leave whatever I do here.'

'That's not f—'

'Fair?' she queried, and turned and shook the loaded toasting fork at him. 'Who's talking fair?'

She was gorgeous, he thought suddenly. She was just... gorgeous. She looked like an avenging angel, in faded serviceable clothes and wielding a toasting fork like a sword. Her cheeks were two bright spots of colour. Her eyes were flashing demons.

He thought...he thought...

He thought he wanted to kiss her.

Dumb move, he told himself desperately. Really, really dumb.

He really, really wanted to kiss her.

'Well?' she demanded and he tried to think what he should be thinking.

'The castle is pure luxury,' he said weakly. 'There's no need for me to stay.'

'I don't want you to stay,' she said, surprising him, 'but as guarantee of the children's safety you must.'

He gazed at her, and she gazed back, meeting his look head-on and not flinching.

He still just wanted to kiss...

'I do what I have to do,' she said. 'Do you?'

'Yes, but—'

'Then it's settled. You'll stay?'

'I need—'

'You'll stay?'

'Yes,' he said, driven against the ropes and acknowledging he had no choice. 'I'll stay in Alp d'Estella, yes.'

'Excellent,' Pippa said and glowered. 'Not that I want you near us, mind. You unsettle me.'

'Do I?' He started to smile, but she raised her toasting fork again.

'I have no idea why you unsettle me and I don't like it,' she told him. 'So stop smiling. It just unsettles me more. And there's only one more stipulation that has to be met.'

'Another!'

'It's the most important.'

'What is it?'

She stared down at her feet. Dolores had rolled over onto her back, exposing her vast stomach to the radiant heat.

'As long as we can figure out the quarantine issues, Dolores comes too. All or none. Take us or leave us.'

He stared down at the ancient mutt—a great brown dog looking like nothing so much as a Hound of the Baskervilles. A sleeping hound of the Baskervilles. 'She'd be happier here.'

'In the middle of winter? Kennelled without us?'

'Most dogs—'

'She's not most dogs. Alice gave me Dolores as a puppy when my mother died. She's been with me ever since—my one true love. Who needs men when I have Dolores?' She retrieved the half-baked crumpet, looked at it with regret and started another. 'Wicked waste.'

'Taking a dog to Alp d'Estella?'

'Interrupting the toasting process. It really messes with the texture. Let's get back to important stuff.'

'Which is?'

'Crumpets.'

'Sure.'

But he still really, really wanted to kiss her.

He didn't. She didn't even guess that he wanted to. Forty-eight hours later Pippa found herself in a first class airline seat somewhere over Siberia, heading for…Alp d'Estella?

There'd been so much to do before she'd left that she'd fallen into an exhausted sleep almost as soon as the plane took off. Now she woke to find the internal lights were off and the light from outside was the dim glow of a northern twilight. Across the aisle Sophie, Claire and Marc were solidly asleep. They'd enjoyed having a seat each at first, but then the twins had bundled in together and Marc had lifted his arm rest so he could join them.

They looked like a litter of well-fed puppies. Down in the hold, Dolores was hopefully sleeping as well, in a padded, warmed crate she'd inspected with caution but deemed fit for travel-snoozing. Kids and dog. Pippa's responsibilities.

Was she putting them at risk? she wondered for about the hundredth time. Surely not. She'd rung the people Max had given as referees and they'd confirmed his story. Max was honourable, they'd said. She'd be safe.

But the kids would be safer at home.

Maybe, but they'd be cold and hungry. With the state of her bank balance she'd been close to needing welfare. And if anything happened to her…

She hadn't succeeded with the farm, she thought miserably, and where was life sending her now? The enormity of what she'd promised eight years ago washed over her, as it had time and time again since Gina's death.

What cost a promise?

'Have you ever thought of walking away from them?' Max asked from right beside her and she jumped about a foot.

She could barely see him. His seat was at a slight incline and hers was out flat. She struggled with some buttons and her seat rose to upright.

She passed him on the way up.

There was a moment's silence while she sat bolt upright and felt stupid. Then he leaned over her and touched her seat control again. Her seat sank smoothly to the same incline as his.

She smelled the masculine smell of him as he leaned over.

Their faces were now six inches apart.

She backed up a little, fast, and she felt his smile rather than saw it. 'Worry not,' he told her. 'I'm no ogre, Pippa, hauling you off to my dark and gloomy castle, to have my wicked way with you.'

'You can hardly have your wicked way when I'm chaperoned by three kids and a dog,' she managed and she tried to relax. But he was still smiling and she was feeling very…very…

Very she didn't know what. If only he weren't so damned good-looking. If only he weren't so…disconcerting.

He was very disconcerting. And mentioning wicked ways hadn't helped a bit. He was so…

Sexy.

There were things stirring inside her that had been repressed for years. She swallowed and told herself that these ideas had to go straight back to being repressed again.

They refused to cooperate.

'Have you left the farm since Gina's death?' he asked and she shook her head.

'You've never wanted to?'

'No. When Alice died, Gina worried there was no extended family. I told her I'd always be there for her kids. It seemed dumb at the time, but I guess that's what most parents do. They worry about protecting their kids for ever.'

'And now you'll look after these kids for ever? That's some promise.'

'Gina and Alice were my family. The kids are my family now.'

'Tell me how that happened? Why were you so close to Gina and her mother?'

She hesitated. There was something about the half-light, the warmth of the pillows and blankets of her bed-cum-seat, and Max's face being six inches from hers, that meant she either had to accept this closeness or withdraw completely.

She'd hardly spoken of her past. But now…

'When she was a kid my mother…drank too much,' she whispered. 'So did Alice.'

'Alice drank?' He frowned. 'Gina's mother? My aunt?'

'Alice used to say it ran in her family,' she whispered. 'The royal side. She had a huge fight with her parents and ended up in Australia. She was wild for a long time. With alcohol. Drugs maybe? I don't know. Anyway she got pregnant and that's when she met my mother. They were both on their own and pregnant and trying to stay clean. They were friends for a bit. After I was born my mother reverted, but Alice never touched a drop from the time she got pregnant. Whenever my mother was so ill she couldn't take care of me, Alice was there. In the end it was like Alice had three children. Gina, me and my mother. Only Gina and I grew up. My mother died when I was twelve.'

'I'm glad Alice was there for you,' Max said, his voice carefully neutral. 'It must have been really tough.'

'It was. But Alice made it less so. She had no support yet she managed to help Gina and I both through nursing. And when Gina met Donald…that was the wedding to end all weddings. It was our happy ever after.'

'But happy ever after is for fairy tales.'

'It is,' she murmured. 'But Alice died after Marc was born—she had an aneurism—thinking we were all happily settled. So she did have her happy ever after.'

'She was broke, though?'

'There was never any money.'

Max frowned. 'Our side of the family always thought she'd married well.'

'I suspect she told her parents that. She just wanted to be shot of them. She hated what the royal family stood for.'

'That makes two of us,' he said bleakly. 'Three counting my mother.' But then he shook his head, as if chastising himself for going down a road he didn't want to pursue.

'But you?' he said gently. 'How can you be happy?'

'I'm happy.'

'Have you ever had a boyfriend?'

Hang on a minute… What had that come from? 'Mind your own business.'

'I'd like to know.'

'You tell me yours, then,' she said astringently. 'And I'll tell you mine.'

'Okay,' he said surprisingly. 'I've had girlfriends.'

She shouldn't ask. But suddenly she was intrigued. 'Not serious?'

'They find out I have money and all of a sudden I'm desirable. It's a great turn-off.'

'That's tough,' she said, but her voice was loaded with irony. 'You know, I was actually engaged to be married when Gina and Donald were killed. Tom thought Dolores was bad enough, but when he found I intended to take the kids he couldn't run fast enough.'

'As you say—tough.'

'No,' she said evenly. 'These kids are my family, as much as if I'd borne them myself. If Tom didn't want them, then it was his problem.' She shrugged and smiled. 'And maybe I don't blame him. Three kids and dogs is a huge ask.'

'It's a huge ask of you.'

Her smile faded. 'Not so much. I love them to bits. And you... If you threaten their happiness—their security—you'll answer to me, Max de Gautier.'

'I'd never do that.'

They fell silent then, but it was a better silence. She felt strangely more at peace than she'd been in a long time. Which was dumb, she told herself. She was heading somewhere she'd never heard of and she had to stay on her guard.

But she wasn't totally responsible. She glanced across at the sleeping children and she thought in a few minutes the stewardess would bring them something to eat and she didn't need to work out how to pay for it.

And she was sitting beside Maxsim de Gautier. Any woman would feel okay sitting beside this man, she thought. There wasn't any chance he might be interested in her—what man would look twice at a woman loaded with three kids, a king-sized debt and a dog?—but she was woman enough to enjoy it while she had it.

'Why does saving Alp d'Estella matter so much to you?' she asked, suddenly curious.

'It just does.'

'No, but why?' she prodded. 'You've been brought up in France. Why do you still care about a little country your father or your grandfather walked away from?'

'I just...do.'

He wasn't telling the truth, she thought. Why? She stared at him, baffled.

'Tell me how you learned to milk cows?' she demanded, moving sideways, and the tension eased a little.

'That's easy. My mother was born on a dairy farm south of Paris. My maternal grandparents still live there. It's run by my uncle now, but it's great. I spent the greater part of my childhood there.'

'Your father's dead.'

The pleasure faded from his voice. 'I didn't have any contact with…either of the men my mother was involved with.'

'And your mother? Where's she?'

'In Paris.'

'When did—Thiérry's father—die?'

'When I was fifteen. I've always referred to him as my father too.'

'When did your brother die?'

'At the same time.'

'They were killed together?'

'In a car crash. Yes.'

'Oh, Max.'

She paused. There were things here she wanted to find out, but she didn't know the right questions. 'Do you build in Paris?' she said at last and he nodded.

'Yes.'

'What sort of buildings?'

'Big ones.'

'Skyscrapers?'

'Yes.'

She blinked. She'd never met anyone who built skyscrapers. 'Do you work for someone?'

'How do you mean?'

'Do you have a boss?'

'I…no. I had a fantastic boss. I became his off-sider but he died three years ago. I took over the firm.'

'So you're the head of a building firm that builds skyscrapers.'

'You could say that.'

'You're very rich?'

'You disapprove?'

'No.' She hesitated. 'Well, maybe I do, but I guess it's handy.'

'It certainly is,' he said, and he smiled.

He needed to cut that out, she thought crossly. She'd just started to focus and, wham, he smiled, and her thoughts scattered to the four winds.

She bit her lip and bulldozed on. 'So this boss… You said you went to a builder and asked him to teach you how to build.'

'I did.'

'But you had money from the royal family?'

'No. My father gambled using the royal name as collateral,' he said. 'It's taken years to get my mother free of debt. Yes, there was an offer to help from the old prince, but my mother would have died rather than accept it.'

'Tell me about the car crash?' she asked, tentatively now, unsure whether she was intruding, but needing to know.

He didn't take offence. It seemed he'd decided to answer as honestly as he could. 'My father was drunk,' he said bluntly. 'The royal curse. But unlike Alice, he didn't fight his addiction. The Alp d'Estella royal family is not a pedigree to be proud of.'

She thought about that for a moment and didn't like what she thought.

'Yet you're propelling Marc into the middle of it?'

'I suspect you'll be strong enough to keep him level-headed.'

'You didn't think that before you knew me,' she reasoned. 'Yet still you wanted Marc to come.'

'I did.' He was silent for a moment, deep in his own thoughts. 'Maybe I hadn't thought things through then, either,' he admitted. 'I knew Marc stood to inherit. I thought he was a child. It couldn't change his life so much, and there's so much at stake. But, yes, I've had qualms since and I've seen that you have the strength to ignore…what the palace can offer.'

She hesitated. 'You can't possibly know that's true.'

'And yet I do.'

'But you?' she said, pushing it further. 'How do I know you don't just want to be Prince Regent for money and power?'

'For the same reason I know you won't be seduced by money

and power,' he said evenly, and lifted her fingers in the dark and held them against the side of his face. 'You know me and I know you.'

She felt…breathless. 'That's just plain dumb.'

'But it's true.'

'It's smooth talking,' she said crossly. She was out of her league and she knew it. 'I'm a nobody and you're Prince Regent.'

'Nobody's a nobody. Don't insult yourself.' And he didn't let go of her hand.

He was a restful man, she thought. He didn't feel the need to fill the silence. He let the silence do the talking for him.

But his hold on her hand was growing more…personal, and she wasn't quite sure the silent bit was all that wise. He was too close.

He was too male.

'So how did you get to own a construction company?' She finally managed to pull her hand away. He let his eyes fall to her fingers, then raised his eyes and smiled with a gentle mockery. He understood what she was doing.

'I told you. I went to—'

'A builder and got a job. How old were you?'

'Fifteen. The farm couldn't support us.'

'Your mother wasn't working?'

'My mother was in the same car crash that killed my father and Thiérry. She's paralysed from the waist down. The farm's not big enough to pay off my father's debts or my mother's medical bills.' He shrugged. 'The builder who employed me was an old friend of my grandparents, so, yes, I did have family connections, but I believe I've more than earned the position I'm in now.'

'So who's paying for these plane tickets?' she asked, frowning. 'You or the Alp d'Estella government?'

'I'll be reimbursed.'

'If this works out.'

'As you say.' His gaze met hers, steady and forthright. But there were things he wasn't telling her, she decided. There were things she had to figure out for herself.

'You need to wash,' he told her, cutting in on her thoughts. 'They'll be bringing breakfast.'

'At four in the afternoon?'

'You're in a whole new world. Welcome to breakfast.'

'I feel dizzy.'

'Just take one step at a time,' he said and touched her face in a gesture of reassurance that shouldn't be enough to send warmth right through her entire body. It shouldn't be enough but it definitely was. Her hand came up instinctively and met his. Once more he grasped her fingers in his and held.

This was a gesture of reassurance, she told herself frantically. No more.

'It'll be okay,' he said.

'Will it?'

'Yes.'

'I don't see how I can fit in. But I won't leave the children.'

'Of course you won't.'

'But to stay in this place…'

The hold on her hand was suddenly compelling. 'Pippa, I won't increase your burden. I promise you that. Let's just take every day as it comes and we'll see what happens.'

'But—'

'It's okay, Pippa.' He stared down at her in the half light, and his grip firmed, strong and sure.

The silence stretched out.

She gazed up at him, waiting…

'Would you mind if I kiss you?' he asked.

Her heart missed a beat. Would she mind?

'No,' she whispered, for some dumb, crazy reason that for ever after she couldn't fathom. But say it she did. For some things were inevitable.

Like the touch of Max's mouth on her lips.

She shouldn't have been expecting it—but she was. She'd been expecting it since that night by the fireside. She'd been… wanting it. And here it was.

The feel of him… The taste of him… The glorious sensation of melting into him in the dim light.

It was a culmination of circumstance, she told herself hazily. It was the warmth of these wonderful seats, after being cold for every waking moment. It was the hazy feeling of having just woken from sleep to find him beside her. It was the softness and luxury of alpaca blankets and goose-down pillows.

More. It was the strength of the man beside her, and the way his smile lit his eyes. It was the strength of his voice as it reassured her. It was the sense of being protected as she'd never been protected.

It was just... Max.

The moment was so seductive that she'd have had to be inhuman not to respond, and of course she responded. Her need was overwhelming. Her face lifted as if compelled, and her lips met his. Her hands rose to hold his face, getting the angle right, deepening the kiss, taking as well as giving...

Losing herself in the wonderment of him.

The kiss went on and on. Endless. It was a drifting, sensuous pleasure that lifted her out of her cloud of indecision and uncertainty and worry, and left nothing but pleasure.

He'd said it was okay. For now she'd believe him. Unwise or not, it was all she could do.

She surrendered herself to the kiss absolutely and in those few magic moments, before reality reasserted itself...well, those few moments were a gift to treasure.

They might be part of an unwise fantasy, but they were magic, all the same.

She was heading for a fairy tale, she thought mistily.

Anything could happen.

Breakfast happened.

'We didn't mean it,' she said breathlessly as the lights went up.

'I meant it,' he said and he smiled.

'Well, I didn't,' she muttered as she took herself off to the bathroom. 'This is just...ridiculous.'

CHAPTER FIVE

THEY got busy after that, which was just as well, and then the plane landed. From the moment the wheels touched the runway, the sensation of being in a fairy tale intensified until Pippa was pinching herself to believe she was awake. Had Max just kissed her? Had she just been transformed, from frog to princess?

Weird.

Normal passengers got to descend the steps from the plane and immerse themselves in the muddle of luggage location and ongoing transport. Not so Pippa and her little family.

For a start as the plane came to a halt there was an announcement. 'Could passengers remain in their seats to allow the Alp d'Estella royal family to leave the plane.'

It took a few disoriented seconds before Pippa realised the royal family was them. That the airline staff were standing in what seemed a guard of honour to welcome them.

The children had been fast asleep as they'd landed and they were still half asleep when they left the plane. Max carried Claire and Sophie, and Pippa led a dazed Marc.

'I don't want Pippa carrying anything,' Max growled to the nearest steward as Pippa went to lift her holdall. 'She's hurt her back. And our very elderly dog is in the hold. Could you locate her as soon as possible, please?'

They were two tiny instances of Max caring, Pippa thought. Her back was better. She'd forgotten it, but Max hadn't.

Pippa, who'd hardly been cared for in her life, felt a sting of tears as she reached the red carpet to find Dolores already being invited to leave her doggy crate. She stooped and hugged her dog, then turned and watched Max juggle a sleepy twin in each arm, and tease Marc a little as they gave her time to reacquaint herself with Dolores.

Tears were dumb. She should be soaking up every single thing. The ladies of Tanbarook would never believe her, she thought, and that made her tears change to a smile. Photographers were everywhere. What would be the reaction if Pippa's face was plastered over the news-stand back in Tanbarook?

'What's funny?' Max asked.

A limousine was waiting at the edge of red carpet, its uniformed chauffeur saluting. Even Dolores looked stunned. Her nose was sniffing the warm air. Sun!

'It's warm,' Marc breathed and stooped to inform Dolores. 'It's warm, Dolores. We're going to a castle and it's warm.'

'I want Tanbarook to see us now,' Pippa whispered and Max chuckled.

'You want a family shot for the tabloids? Marc, hold Pippa's hand and lean against me. Leave Dolores there—we'll arrange ourselves around her.' Max edged close to Pippa, and before she knew it he'd organised them into a tight shot.

'Smile,' he told Pippa.

'Why?' She was astounded.

'We're the closest thing this country has to a royal family. Tanbarook *is* going to see you. Smile.'

She managed a weakish sort of smile but she was so confused her head was threatening to spin off. 'I'm not family,' she muttered, staring down at Dolores, who was licking Max's boots. 'Isn't Dolores supposed to go into quarantine until she's vet-checked?'

'We had a vet check her before she left. She's a royal dog now. And you're as royal as I am. We're royal by association. The royal family.'

He was smiling at her as photographers snapped around her and she felt her color rising by the minute. 'I should be like the governess, standing ten steps back.'

'Same with me. But you won't let me leave, and if you leave the kids and Dolores will howl.'

'I wouldn't,' Marc said, affronted. 'But Dolores might,' he conceded.

'There you go. Smile,' he ordered again. 'Pippa, there's only one thing worse than publicity, and that's publicity when you're glowering. It makes you look like you're constipated.'

She choked. 'Gee, thanks.'

'I just thought I'd mention it. So smile.'

'I'm smiling,' she said through gritted teeth. 'And neither the kids or Dolores are scared of you. They think you're the next best thing to Father Christmas.'

'Little they know.'

'There's the ogre side of you as well?'

'I'm not exactly a family man.'

'Why not?' It was out before she thought about it—a direct response to something she needed to know. To something that had to be sorted before she took one step further.

And Max's smile faded.

Why not? he wondered, as the cameras clicked around them and he tried to resurrect his smile. Why had he never taken that last step? From lover to husband...

Marriages were fraught. His mother's marriage had led to irretrievable disaster. 'Don't ever marry,' she'd said to him over and over. 'You can't ever know how someone will turn out. Oh, Max, take lovers, do what you need to be happy, but be so careful...'

He'd hardly decided not to marry because of his mother's experiences, but then, it had made him so careful that such a decision had almost been made for him.

'You're not gay, are you?' Pippa asked thoughtfully and his thoughts hit a brick wall. He turned and stared at her. Stunned.

'What did you say?'

'Smile,' she reminded him. The photographers were clicking from every angle. 'I was asking whether you're gay.'

'Didn't I just kiss you?'

'That's proof you're not gay?'

'Yes,' he said, revolted. 'It wasn't a platonic kiss.'

'No,' she said thoughtfully, 'but then I didn't really inspect it for platonic. Maybe I wouldn't recognise it if I saw it. I lead a very sheltered life.'

She was teasing him, he thought. She was trying to get him to react, here and now, in front of the country's press.

'Shut up,' he said, carefully pasting on his smile and carefully no longer looking at her. 'One more word, Phillippa Donohue, and I'll set the twins down and teach you what a platonic kiss isn't.'

'In front of everyone? You wouldn't dare.'

'No,' he said, sounding regretful. 'You're right. I wouldn't. But only because it'd make our lives even more complicated than they already are. Which is very complicated indeed.'

Okay, so that little interlude made her flustered. The stilted welcome speech made by an official made her more flustered still. And the ride from airport to castle, in the back of the limousine with Max in the seat opposite, the children snoozing beside them and Dolores draped over their feet, made her even more flustered.

'That was a dumb thing to do,' she managed about ten minutes after they'd left the airport, which was the time it had taken to figure anything at all to say.

'What was?'

'You kissing me.'

'I didn't kiss you in front of the photographers,' he said virtuously. 'I wanted to but I had my arms full of twins.'

'You kissed me on the plane.'

'That was necessary. Because I suspected that you suspected I was gay. And I was right. Not that my kiss seemed to reassure you.'

'It reassured me,' she said hastily and went back to staring out the car window.

The scenery was amazing.

She'd read about these four tiny countries. There'd been a fuss in the Australian press when Pippa's countrywoman had married the Crown Prince of Alp d'Azuri. There'd also been a write-up and potted history of how these countries had come to be, and she'd found time to reread it on the internet before she'd come.

A king in a large neighbouring country, way back in the sixteenth century, had had five sons. The boys had grown up warring and the old king had foreseen ruin as the sons had vied for the Crown.

So he'd pre-empted trouble. He'd carved four separate countries from his southern border, and told his younger sons that the cost of their own principality was lifelong allegiance to their oldest brother.

His plan hadn't worked, the article had told her. Granting whole counties to men with a lust for war was hardly a guarantee of wise rule. The four princes and their descendants had brought four wonderful countries to the brink of ruin.

Ruin? Pippa stared out of the car window and saw lush river valleys, towering mountains, quaint cottages, herds of cream and white cows, the odd goat, tiny settlements that might almost have come from a photograph from a hundred years before. It didn't look...ruined.

'It's beautiful,' she breathed.

'If you like postcards,' Max said shortly. 'But the reality's less than beautiful. You were cold and hungry this winter. These people are cold and hungry every winter.'

She glowered again, suspecting pressure. 'Don't you dare show me starving peasants. I won't be responsible.'

'I couldn't anyway,' he conceded. 'It's summer and the harvest this year will be a good one. Things are okay at the moment.'

'But not for long?'

'Yes, for long. If we can pull this off.' He looked down at the sleeping Marc and his mouth quirked.

'I won't—'

'No. You agree to nothing. Let's just see how it goes. Meanwhile if you look to your right you'll see the castle...now.'

'Oh.'

As an exclamation it was totally inadequate, but it was all she could think of. Built into the side of one of the towering alps, the castle was a mass of gleaming white stone, set against the purple of the mountains behind. She stared out, stunned, as the castle grew larger against its magnificent backdrop. It was all turrets, battlements and towers, like something straight out of a fairy story.

She nudged Marc, but he'd settled back into sleep. They were now in the middle of the children's night and the future Crown Prince of Alp d'Estella had drifted back where he belonged.

Frustrated, she bent over to wake the twins, but Max caught her hand.

'Leave them. They'll see enough of it in the future.'

There was something in his voice that caught her. She stared across at him, and then turned and looked again at the castle. The battlements seemed to be looming above them, towering over the tiny town nestled underneath.

'You don't like it,' she said.

'I don't like what it represents.'

'What does it represent?'

'Too much power. Too much money by too few people.'

'You're rich yourself.'

'I earned my money through hard work,' he said shortly. 'The princes in this place got their money by taxing their people until they bled. You'd think I'd have anything to do with that?'

She thought about it, wondering. Thinking back to the family tree.

'Your grandfather left the palace and went to France?'

'Yes. But he's not really my grandfather.'

'So you've had no contact with the palace?'

'I…no.'

'Does that mean maybe?'

'My…my father did,' Max said shortly. 'More fool him.'

'You blame the palace for what happened to your father? And to Thiérry?'

'My mother does and she should know.'

'Right,' Pippa said and cast an uneasy glance down at Marc. This was getting tricky. 'So if Marc takes on the Crown you'll hold Thiérry's death against him?'

'That's ridiculous.'

'As ridiculous as staring out at that great hunk of stone and saying that's what killed your brother?'

'I didn't say—'

'No, but you meant,' she said. 'I look at that castle and think fairy tale. But you look and see a dead brother. A psychologist could have a field-day with that.'

'A field-day!'

'Yes, you know—a day when everything's on show. Like your emotions now.'

'They're not on show.'

'No?'

'No.'

She grinned. She had the great Maxsim de Gautier flummoxed. Excellent.

'This is serious,' he told her.

'Nonsense,' she said soundly, beginning to relax. 'This is fun.'

It might have fun potential but it was so grand it took her breath away.

The limousine swept inside the castle grounds and pulled to a halt in a vast forecourt ringed by fountains. The chauffeur moved swiftly, opening the door for them, even saluting.

Ignoring Max's protest—her back really was better—she gathered the nearest twin—Claire—into her arms and climbed out. At the sight of what lay ahead she gasped. She stared around her for a couple of awed moments while her stomach sank at the enormity of where she'd found herself.

There were thirty or more servants forming a guard of honour to the grand front entrance—vast marble steps set between marble columns flanking doors wide enough to accommodate a Sherman tank. The servants were dressed as the type of domestic servants Pippa had seen on television. The women were in severe black with frilled white aprons and white caps. The men were in total black, or, even more amazingly, red and black livery.

'You're kidding?' Pippa breathed to Max. 'This is something out of a movie.'

'These people take royalty seriously,' Max said severely, and Pippa gulped and nodded, stifling an inappropriate desire to giggle.

'I can see that they do.'

A middle-aged man was standing apart from the servants, dressed in what looked like a military uniform, heavily decorated.

He was big and heavy set, with a handle-bar moustache that made Pippa want to giggle again.

'Welcome home, Your Highness,' he told Max in careful English and Max winced.

'I'm not Your Highness until I'm sworn in as Regent, and this is not my home.' He gestured to Marc who was stirring into wakefulness in his arms. He set Marc onto his feet and reached back into the car to collect Sophie. 'This is the new Crown Prince of Alp d'Estella and his sisters. I'd like to take them straight to the nursery. It's been prepared?'

'Of course.' The man looked at Marc for a long moment, an enigmatic expression on his face. Then he shrugged and turned his attention to Pippa. 'This would be the children's nanny?'

'I'm their guardian,' Pippa said, more firmly than she felt, and she clutched Claire so hard that the little girl muttered a protest.

'I see,' the man said, assessing her from her toes up. She was wearing faded jeans and a comfortable windcheater. Max should have warned her, she thought, starting to feel vaguely hysterical. She needed a tiara or six. 'We'll prepare a bedroom for you in the Queen's wing,' the man said and she forgot about tiaras.

'Where are the children sleeping?'

'In the nursery.'

'Is that in the Queen's wing?'

'No, but—'

'I sleep where the children sleep,' she said. 'Isn't that right, Max?'

'Of course it is,' Max said. 'Pippa, this is Carver Levout. Carver is Chief of Staff here. Carver, this is Miss Phillippa Donohue, the children's guardian. Whatever Pippa says regarding the children's welfare goes.'

'Yes, sir,' the man said woodenly, but the glance he gave Pippa wasn't wooden. It was appraising. It made Pippa stop feeling like giggling. She shivered.

'You'll be fine here,' Max said bracingly. 'Carver will introduce you to the staff and they'll look after you. I guess you'll all need to sleep. I'll carry the kids up to their bed before I leave.'

She froze. 'Before you go where?'

'To a hotel down in the village. I'll check with you tomorrow that you have everything you need.'

He was the picture of innocence, she thought. His nerve was breathtaking. 'Excuse me, but you're staying here,' she managed.

'As I agreed to,' he said smoothly. 'In the hotel in the village.'

'You're staying at the castle.'

'I never said—'

'You did,' she said, more bluntly than was polite but she wasn't feeling polite. She was damned if she was going to be left alone with...Carver? What sort of name was that? He even waxed his moustache, she thought. Urk.

They were all waiting for Max to reply. Pippa and thirty servants and Carver. 'Pippa, I'm hardly going far,' Max said reasonably. 'I'm five minutes' drive away. I said I'd stay in Alp d'Estella. I didn't say I'd stay at the castle.'

He was talking to her as if she were dumb. Right, she thought. She was fine with dumb. But it was going to be dumb and stubborn. Without a word she climbed back into the car with Claire, settled the twin on the seat beside her before holding her hands out for Sophie. 'Marc, pop back in the car, love. We're all staying where Mr de Gautier is staying.'

Max looked taken aback. They all looked taken aback. Except Dolores who hadn't shifted out of the car yet. 'Pardon?' Max demanded.

'You heard. Where you stay, we stay.'

'Why?'

'Not because you kissed me,' she muttered, lowering her voice so the assembled reception committee couldn't hear. 'But because this place gives me the heebie-jeebies. I'm not royal. I'm not staying here.'

'That's ridiculous. You don't need to be royal to stay.'

'Neither do you have to be a commoner to go. But if you're going, then I'm going. You got me here under false pretences.'

'I didn't.'

'You did.' She glanced again at the rows of servants and she quailed. There wasn't much that spooked Pippa Donohue, but she was spooked now. She hugged Sophie too hard, and the child muttered a sleepy protest. 'Max, I mean what I say,' she said, trying not to sound belligerent. Trying to sound matter-of-fact. 'Hush, Sophie, we're nearly home. Max says it's just five minutes' drive away.'

Max stared down at her, baffled. 'You have to stay here.'

'You're going to make me, how?'

'It's ridiculous.'

'It is, isn't it?' she agreed. 'You said you'd stay.'

'I didn't.'

'If you didn't then it's semantics and you tricked me. I don't like being tricked.'

'Pippa, I can't stay here.'

'Then neither can we.' She looked behind him. 'You know, everyone's listening to this. It's pretty undignified, don't you think? If I were you I'd come to a decision, and there's only one decision to reach.'

'I don't want to stay in this place,' he told her. He'd tried to make his voice matter-of-fact, but it didn't work. She heard a tinge of desperation behind it, and it almost moved her. But then Pippa glanced down at the child in her arms, at Marc who was looking confused, at Claire on the seat beside her and at Dolores at her feet.

Then she looked at Moustache. She didn't know why but Carver Levout made her nervous and she had nothing to go on here but her instincts. She was responsible for this little family. She couldn't afford to be swayed by Max's desperation.

'If there are reasons you can't stay here, then they hold true for us all,' she whispered. 'If I'd known you were afraid to stay then I'd never have agreed to come.'

'I'm not afraid.'

'Then what are you?'

'I just…hate it.'

'That's just as bad.'

'Pippa—'

'It's only stone and wood and thirty or so servants. Oh, and I hear tell it has three swimming pools. So if it's not scary, it might be fun.'

'But Thiérry…' He stopped short. His brother's name was an involuntary exclamation, Pippa thought, and she wondered why.

'Where does Thiérry come into this?'

'He doesn't.' He pressed his lips closed as though that was the end of the matter. She stared up at him for a moment and then thought maybe that was a plan. She pressed her own lips together and looked straight ahead.

Standoff.

She hadn't counted on Sophie. She'd stirred into wakefulness in Pippa's arms, wriggled until she could see and she'd looked beyond Max to the castle. 'We're here,' she said sleepily. 'It's just like my picture books. But bigger. Why aren't we getting out of the car? Claire, Claire, wake up.'

Right on cue Claire woke. 'We're here?' she demanded. 'We're at the castle?'

'Yes, but Pippa won't let us stay,' Marc said, trying to figure it out. ''Cos Max won't stay and she's scared of all these people.'

'She's not scared,' Max said shortly. 'She's just pigheaded.'

'There's two of us being pigheaded,' she told him. 'And I'm not backing down.'

'Hell, Pippa—'

'You stay or we go.'

'You could all go.' It was Carver, standing behind them, listening intently.

'We're all staying,' Max snapped.

She stared at him. She'd won, she thought, but it didn't feel like winning. What was it that he was afraid of?

But Carver was waiting. He had to have an answer, and she wasn't going to let him see she was rattled. 'Then that's settled,' she said smoothly. 'Okay, we all need to be introduced. Sophie, you take one of Max's hands and, Claire, you take the other. Marc, you walk in front. You guys go along the row of people here and find out who everyone is.'

'You need to be introduced too,' said Marc.

'I'm not royal,' Pippa said. 'I'll come up behind and bow and scrape to anyone above second footman.'

'This isn't a joke,' Max snapped.

'It's not,' she agreed, but she smiled. Only she knew the effort it cost her. 'But neither is it Greek tragedy. Let's make this fun, Max. Let's go.'

Max had no intention of making it fun. He was stiffly formal, right up until they were shown the nursery and left alone.

'You rest,' he said. 'I'll see you at dinner.'

'If you leave the palace, then we're out of here, even if we have to walk,' Pippa warned him, still trying to sound pigheaded but suspecting she just sounded intimidated. Liveried footmen had deposited their sad-looking luggage in a dressing room big enough to hold clothes for a small army. A couple of maids were unpacking. At the thought of the scant possessions they were unpacking Pippa felt like sinking.

She shouldn't be clutching at Max, she thought, but she had no choice. He was her lifeline to her other life.

'You've made that clear,' Max said stiffly. 'But the children need rest and so do I. I'll see you at dinner.'

'Um, don't leave me,' she muttered but he was already turning away.

She was alone. With three kids and two maids and a dog.

There was too much to think of here. All she wanted to think of was Max. She wanted to run after him. She'd hurt him by insisting he stayed here, she thought, but what was she to do?

The casual friendliness was gone, replaced by a stiff formality she couldn't understand.

Where was the man who had kissed her?

She couldn't run after him, and she had to forget the kiss. That was just a dopey thing to do in the dark on the plane, she told herself, but there was a part of her that was saying it was no such thing. It wasn't just a kiss.

Yes, it was.

Whatever, she told herself harshly. There was no time for wondering about Max now.

They were in a vast school-room-cum-sitting room, with desks at one end and huge settees around a fire at the other end. It was hardly cold enough to warrant a fire, but Dolores headed straight to it and Pippa looked at the logs piled high at the side with longing. If she could transport those to Tanbarook...

What else? There were doors leading off the main room, and the kids were opening them. They led to individual bedrooms, each with a massive four-poster bed.

'Wow,' said Marc. He approached the first bed with caution. It was six feet or more across and almost three feet high, hung with crimson velvet and gold brocade. Marc clambered up and tugged the twins up to join him.

The three kids wriggled into the pile of pillows mounded against the bed head, like puppies exploring a new basket. 'It's really soft,' Sophie called wonderingly, giving a tentative bounce. 'Pippa, will you sleep here with us?'

'Sure,' she said.

'Excuse me, miss,' one of the maids—the oldest one?—said, in tentative English.

'I speak your language,' Pippa said, trying out her language skills. To her delight it seemed to work. The woman's face relaxed a little and she reverted. 'Well, then... Mr Levout said we were to show you to the bedroom at the end of this wing.'

'I'm not sure why Mr Levout thinks it's important, but I'm sleeping here.'

There was a touch of hand-wringing at that. It seemed an effort to say it, but the woman finally succeeded. 'Mr Levout won't like it.' It sounded like a threat.

'Then the kids can sleep in the bedroom Mr Levout chose for me. We'll all sleep there.'

There were three gasps of dismay from under the mound of pillows, and two gasps of dismay from the maids. 'Mr Levout will think it's inappropriate.'

'I'll explain it to Mr Levout.'

'You can't.' They looked afraid, Pippa thought incredulously. Why?

'I'll explain it's nothing to do with you. I'll tell him it's just me being pigheaded.'

'Miss, we'll get into trouble if we don't do what Mr Levout wishes.'

Trouble? These two were well past retirement age, Pippa thought. What could Levout do? Sack them? Surely they'd be looking forward to retirement anyway.

She took a deep breath. She was probably only here for a month, she thought, so there was no need to make trouble when it could be avoided. But if, she thought, *if* Marc did end up as Crown Prince, then the ground rules had to be set now. Even if these two were about to retire.

'I gather Marc...' She caught herself. 'I gather His Highness, Prince Marc, is to be the new Crown Prince of Alp d'Estella. I'm his legal guardian. Any decision regarding the children will thus be made by me. Not by Mr Levout. Not by anyone else. Do I make myself clear?'

Two jaws sagged.

'Well?'

'Oh, my dear,' the oldest woman said, and she beamed. 'Oh, yes, miss.'

'You ought to stand up to him,' the other woman breathed. 'No one else does.' She looked to where the kids were enthusiastically bouncing on their four-poster. 'He'd have a heart attack if he saw that.'

Pippa turned and looked at the kids. They'd tugged off their shoes before bouncing. As guardian, could she demand anything more? 'They're allowed to bounce,' she said.

'Oh, yes, miss,' the oldest maid breathed and she chuckled. 'I have a grandson who loves bouncing.'

'You have a grandson?'

'I have three.'

'Excuse me, but why are you still working as a maid?'

There was blank incomprehension. 'We need to,' the woman said at last. 'Jobs are scarce.'

'You don't have pensions?'

'Pensions?'

'Well,' Pippa said and set her shoulders. 'Maybe it's just as well we came after all.'

What was she saying?

* * *

The maids left soon after and they were left alone.

The children bounced. They explored every inch of the nursery. Then the four of them—Dolores excused herself as she'd found a fire—took themselves further, checking school rooms, bedroom upon bedroom, living rooms, libraries, great halls, ballrooms… They knocked at each door and when there was no response they peered inside.

They grew more and more awed.

They found the inside swimming pool. It was huge, with a special lap lane designed with wave blockers so the water stayed calm all the time.

'I want a swim,' Marc breathed.

'Tomorrow.' Pippa gazed round with awe. 'Let's go outside and see if we can find the other two pools.'

'Where is everyone?' Marc asked. 'All those people.'

'Below stairs, I guess,' Pippa said, giving a nervous giggle. 'That's what they say on telly about where the servants live. But take no notice of me. I'm guessing.'

'Should we go downstairs and say hello?'

'I guess we said hello when we arrived,' Pippa said cautiously. 'I'm not too sure anyone wants to say hello after that. Let's go outside. It seems…safer.'

CHAPTER SIX

MAX spent two hours with Levout, which were two hours more than he wanted to spend with the man, but there were practicalities to work out. If he was stuck here then he might as well sort them out now. He emerged from the castle offices feeling vaguely tainted. He hated being related to this family. So many wrongs…

But at least now they could be sorted. He'd watched Levout trying to hide dismay as he'd gone through the initial changes he wanted instigated, and he thought, You don't know the half of it. These were just palace changes. Tomorrow he'd start looking wider.

But now he was starting to be nervous about Pippa's whereabouts. She'd threatened she'd leave if he didn't stick around and he knew her well enough to realise she'd carry through with a threat. If she thought he was no longer in the castle…

He'd check. She'd probably be resting, he decided, and he headed for the nursery, climbing the vast staircase three stairs at a time.

The nursery was empty.

He rang the bell and an elderly housemaid appeared, looking apprehensive.

'Where are the children?' he asked.

'They're with Pippa. I mean…Miss Phillippa.'

'Did she ask you to call her Pippa?'

'Oh, yes,' the woman said, and her nervousness disappeared in a smile. 'I said to call me Beatrice but she said I was old enough to be her mother and she'd only call me Beatrice if I called her Pippa. She said that goes for all the staff, but we talked about it and thought maybe we wouldn't call her that in front of Mr Levout.'

'Very wise.' What was the gossip below stairs? he wondered. They probably knew more than he did. 'Is she in her room?' he asked.

'She says she's sleeping here in the nursery.'

He stared at the enormous nursery. It was more like a gallery than a nursery, he thought. If he'd been stuck in here as a kid, alone, he'd have had nightmares. Maybe Pippa was right. But...

'Are there enough beds?'

'There are five bedrooms. But Pippa says they only need one.'

'That's ridiculous.'

'Yes, sir.'

He looked at Beatrice, who looked back at him, expressionless.

'You don't agree?'

'I have grandchildren,' she said gently. 'If one of them was the new Crown Prince, maybe I'd be sleeping with him, too. And maybe the dog as well.'

She met his gaze, without a hint of a smile.

'You're saying it's unsafe.'

'No, sir. At least... ' She hesitated. 'Sir, I'm only a maid. But if it was my child who was Crown Prince, I'd hold him close.'

'Because...'

'I couldn't say, sir,' she said softly, turning back to her unpacking, leaving him vaguely worried. What was she telling him?

He'd promised Pippa they'd be safe. Was he sure? He thought back to Levout's concerns. A lot of petty officialdom stood to lose substantial income if what Max planned came to pass.

Yeah, but they'd had a prince on the throne for four hundred years. Surely they couldn't object—or do anything about it if they did object?

All the same, suddenly he thought that Pippa and Dolores sleeping with Marc wasn't such a bad idea.

That worried him as well.

Dammit, these weren't Pippa's children. Here he was, asking her to be responsible again.

Where was she?

'They were on the south lawn a little time ago,' Beatrice offered. 'They were playing in the fountain.'

The fountain? The huge marble monstrosity with dragons and warriors fighting it out on the front lawn?

He crossed to the French windows and stared down at the fountain-cum-sculpture in the middle of the immaculately mani-cured lawn.

There was no Pippa and no children but beside the fountain was a muddle of discarded clothes, and a patch of pristine lawn had been muddied.

Beatrice walked over to the window and peered where he was peering.

'Our head gardener treats every blade of grass as a treasure. To let the children muddy it…'

'You think he'll be angry?' Max stared at the mud in bemuse-ment. 'Whipping at dawn? You've met Pippa.'

'I've met Pippa,' the woman said and she ventured a cautious smile. 'Maybe you're right. Maybe he won't be angry. It's so wonderful to have children in the palace again. Maybe she has enough joy in her to charm even the gardening staff.'

She did. By the time Max reached the offending puddle the head gardener, a man in his seventies, was on his knees, care-fully washing mud from the lawn. Before Max could reach him, another man appeared with half a dozen planks.

'What's going on?' he asked, expecting complaints, but none was forthcoming.

'Miss Pippa and the children enjoyed the fountain,' the gardener said mildly. 'So we thought we'd build a small deck so they could get in and out without muddying the lawn.'

A deck. For a fountain where there were swimming pool alternatives.

'Did you tell them about the swimming pools?'

'Oh, yes,' the gardener said and he chuckled. 'The lady asked would I prefer to paddle in a normal pool or duck in and out of dragons. I'd never thought of it like that. But, yes, I could see her point.'

This was amazing. After only two hours in the castle Pippa was already instigating changes. And making friends. Max glanced cautiously around, thinking of Carver Levout. Chief of this whole administration. 'Has Mr Levout given the okay?' he asked.

'No, sir, he hasn't,' the man told him, hauling his cap from his head in a gesture of deference. 'But Miss Pippa said we could refer this to you. She said as Prince Regent you're in charge now. Miss Pippa says she's sure you'll agree. Do you not, sir? Do you want us to stop?'

He didn't want anything. He surely didn't want to be so enmeshed in the workings of this place that he had to think about things like decking.

He had no intention of being hands-on in this place. There might be issues with how Carver ran the palace but he was competent, and Max intended to save his energy for the big battles.

'Where is she now?' he asked, and if his voice was a bit grim he couldn't help it.

'Miss Pippa saw the cows coming in to be milked,' the gardener said. 'I believe they've gone to the dairy to help. Sir, do you wish us to stop building the decking?'

What the heck? 'You've started now. You might as well continue.'

The man smiled. 'Yes, sir,' he said.

Pippa and the children were indeed in the dairy, perched on a top rail overlooking the cows going into the bails. The twins and Marc were dressed in knickers and nothing else. Pippa was in jeans and a T-shirt. Her jeans were rolled up to the knees and her T-shirt was knotted under her breasts, leaving her midriff bare. They were all dripping wet.

They saw him and they waved him to come closer. No sound, though. They knew their cows.

'Hi,' Pippa whispered. 'I thought this'd be really foreign but it's just like home. Without Peculiar.'

Peculiar. He thought back to the cow who'd be even now causing trouble in Bert's yard. 'I bet there's another Peculiar here,' he said darkly. 'There always is.'

'There isn't,' she said. 'I've been talking to the guys here and they're saying these girls are really placid. I'm thinking we might take a few test-tubes home.'

'Test-tubes?'

'For cross-cultural fertilization,' she said patiently. 'Don't you think that'd be ace?'

'We might get some calves just like these,' Marc said. The kids were glowing, high on warmth and good food and fun and excitement. They'd been good-looking kids back in Australia, Max thought, but now he looked at their beaming faces and he felt a twinge of…pride? They hadn't complained once, he thought. He'd seen them tired and hungry and right out of their comfort zone but still they giggled and looked out on life as an adventure. Marc would make a great prince.

Pippa had done a wonderful job of raising them.

Would she agree that they stay?

'Nothing's decided,' Pippa said before he could open his mouth.

'How the hell do you know what I'm thinking?'

'I can see it. I look in your eyes and I see this plus this plus this equals…ooh, let's see…sixty-seven? And then you open your mouth and out it comes. Sixty-seven. Easy.'

He didn't like that it was easy. He was feeling more and more confused.

'Well, how do you understand what these guys are saying?' he asked. 'And the gardener. How did you talk him into building decking?'

'He's building decking?'

'To protect his grass.'

'What a sweetie.'

'You talk French? I didn't know you spoke French?'

'I talk a type of French,' she said. 'I've always been told it's a hybrid, some sort of rural dialect. Now I've discovered where it comes from.' She beamed. 'Here. Well, of course it makes sense, but how lucky's that?'

'I don't understand.'

'Alice,' she said simply. Then, as he looked even more confused, she explained. 'Alice left her family when she was little more than a kid. She got into trouble, she ended up having Gina and being stuck with me, and she made the best of our life together. But there must have been a part of her that was homesick, for every night she'd read to the two of us in her own language. It became fun—it was Gina's and my secret language when we were at school. After Gina got married we had to stop— Donald kept thinking we were talking about him—but it's still a part of me. Finding there's a whole country that speaks it is a joy.'

'It's fun,' Marc said in the same language, and Max stared.

'The kids too?'

'Gina started it with Marc, maybe to make Alice happy. I kept it up. It's always seemed comforting. Some sort of a link. And now we know who we're linked to.'

Wow. He'd brought back family who spoke the language. The enormity of this almost took his breath away.

His task was suddenly a thousand per cent easier.

'Why didn't you tell me?'

'You didn't speak it to us. I honestly didn't know what it was until I heard it here.'

'I do speak it,' he said, switching effortlessly. 'My mother... well, there was an insistence that Thiérry learned it and it was easier for us to practise together.'

She frowned and tugged the two little bodies on either side of her closer so they couldn't topple off the rail. 'So we speak the language—sort of. Why does that make you relieved? I can understand pleased, but not relieved.'

'I was just pleasantly surprised.'

'And relieved.'

'You can't read my feelings.'

'Yes, I can.'

'Then don't,' he snapped, and the cow nearest him swerved his head and gave him a reproachful look.

'Shh,' Sophie whispered. 'We have to be quiet until the cows get to know us.'

'I wonder if I can help milk,' Pippa said.

'You surely don't want to.'

'No.' She peeped a smile. 'But it might make Mr Levout happier. He obviously thinks I'm one of the workers.'

'He's got another think coming. Speaking of which…he's having dinner with us tonight.'

'Really?'

'Really.'

'Eggs and toast in the nursery?'

'Don't push your luck. Do you have anything to wear to a formal dinner?'

She stared. She looked down at her dripping jeans and her bare feet.

She giggled.

'Sure,' she said. 'As formal as you like. I'll wear my dry jeans.'

'Pippa…'

'Don't fret,' she said. The rail they were perched on was four feet high. He was standing right beside her, so she was just above his head height. She reached out and ran her fingers through his hair, an affectionate ruffle such as one she might have given Marc. Or Sophie or Claire. So there was no need for him to react…as he did. 'I won't disgrace you,' she said.

'I know that,' he said stiffly and moved away.

'I won't do anything else either,' she told him, quite kindly. 'There's no need to back off like a frightened horse.'

'I did not!'

'Yes, you did,' Marc said. 'Don't you like it when Pippa rubs your head?'

'No. Yes. I…'

'He doesn't like getting his feathers ruffled, kids,' she told them, turning her attention back to the cows. 'Leave him be to settle. What time's dinner, Mr de Gautier?'

'Seven. The kids will be fed at six. And before you say you and the kids are sticking together, Beatrice, the older of the two maids in the children's wing, will sit with the children. If they give the slightest sign of needing you she'll fetch you. But by the amount of excitement they've had today I suspect they'll be well asleep.'

'So might I be.'

'You slept for fifteen hours on the plane. I've got a crink on my shoulder to prove it.'

'On your shoulder?'

'Where your head landed. You fell sideways.'

'I did not.'

'No, you didn't,' he agreed cordially and she glowered.

'How can I fall sideways in a first class seat?' she demanded.

'You wriggle in your sleep.'

'Well, you snore.'

'I don't!'

'Oh, yes, you do. We need an independent arbitrator. Failing that I refuse to accept responsibility for your crink.'

'I accept your lack of responsibility,' he said and grinned. 'But about dinner. You think you might stay awake until seven?'

'I'm pretty hungry,' she told him. 'But I guess I can always pinch a toast finger from the kids to keep me going.'

She was gorgeous.

Max left them and walked slowly back to the castle entrance, past the gardeners busily erecting their decking, past the pile of kids' clothing…

The castle had subtly changed already.

She was gorgeous.

They were all great, he told himself hastily. The kids and Pippa would breathe new life into this place. He just had to persuade them to stay and things would be fine. The kids could have a glorious time. The load of responsibility would be lifted from Pippa's shoulders and he could leave and get on with his life.

For the first time since he'd been approached after Bernard's death, the awful feeling of being trapped was lessening.

Okay, he still needed to be Regent. He'd accepted that. But back in Paris his construction company was waiting, and in four short weeks he could be back there. He could keep on with the work he loved. He could cope with the legalities of the regency from a distance. He could stay low-key. Okay, he'd accept a bit of publicity now as he persuaded Pippa to keep the children here, but after that he could disappear into the background.

His mother need never be brought into it. It was a solution that suited them all. It felt great.

Or it should feel great. There was one little niggle.

The children's safety?

That was crazy. The maid hadn't said outright she was worried. He was reading too much into it.

Pippa would keep things safe.

And there was another niggle.

Pippa was gorgeous.

So what?

So he wanted to kiss her. He'd already kissed her and it had felt excellent. He wanted, quite desperately, to kiss her again.

Which was dumb. Even one kiss was dumb. Even though for him it had been a light-hearted bit of fun—it must have been—she might not have thought of it as that.

Of course she had. She'd giggled. She'd ruffled his hair then as she'd ruffle one of the kids' hair. She was beginning to hold him in some sort of affection, he thought. She was starting to think of him as family.

Which was good.

Except…did he want her to see him as family? Even that was too close. She'd bulldozed him into staying here for a month and that was a month too long.

He should telephone his mother and let her know what was happening.

Not yet, he thought. He needed to get things sorted first.

What sorted?

It was his thoughts that needed sorting, he decided. His normally razor-sharp intellect was fogged with one sprite of a red-headed woman in soggy jeans and with a bare midriff.

A red-headed woman…

'Excuse me, sir.' He'd been walking up the vast steps to the castle entrance, but as soon as he walked through the doors he found a deputation waiting. Two footmen, carrying boxes. One ancient retainer in topcoat and tails. 'Can you spare a moment?'

He stopped and frowned. 'You are?'

'I'm Blake, sir,' the man said, in the country's mix of French and Italian but with a heavy English accent. 'I was valet to the last prince, and to his father before him.'

'The devil you are.' Max's eyebrows rose. 'They really had valets?'

'Yes, Your Highness. I knew your mother,' he added gently. 'And your father.'

'Right.' Max had his measure now and he'd recalled information he'd read just that afternoon. The castle was full of people like Blake. Blake had been on the castle payroll for sixty years, but the death of the last prince had left no provision for retirement. Long-serving staff had been paid peanuts for years. Unless they stayed working here they'd be destitute.

He'd get reparation under way tomorrow, he thought, watching the old man take one of the parcels from the footman. His hands were shaking as if he had early Parkinson's.

'This is your dress regalia,' the old man said, handling the box with reverence. 'When you flew in before going to Australia you left some clothes behind and we took the liberty of taking measurements and having this made. It would mean a lot to the staff if you were to wear it tonight, the first night of the new order in this Court. Your Highness.'

He lifted the lid with reverence and held it out.

Max stared at Blake. Then he stared down at the box as if he'd just been handed a box of scorpions.

'Dress regalia.'

'As befits the Prince…Regent. You know, we were concerned that the monarchy would disintegrate,' Blake explained. 'But today there's been children's laughter on the lawn and it's not just the staff who are deeply thankful. It's all of the country. But this little prince is only eight years old. We're not so foolish that we think he can possibly rule. You've agreed to be Prince Regent and that means for the next thirteen years you're the country's ruler.' He hesitated. 'As you should be,' he added softly. 'Starting tonight.'

'No, I—'

'Levout says you'll be a puppet ruler,' the old man said, more softly this time, so softly that the two footmen behind him couldn't hear. 'We desperately don't want that to happen.'

'I'll stay in control from a distance.'

'From France?'

'Yes.'

The man's rheumy old eyes misted. 'Sir, that won't work.'

'Of course it will work.'

'This country needs you. For measures to be put in place… well, the people in charge here have been in charge for a very long time.'

'I'll be in close contact.'

'Your Highness…' The man fell silent. There was laughter from outside. Max looked out to where Pippa and the kids were collecting their clothes in readiness to come inside. The children were playing some sort of keepings-off game, and clothes were going everywhere. Pippa was dodging about on the grass, barefooted, laughing, grabbing Marc and hauling him up to whiz him round and round until he shrieked with delight, then setting him down and chasing a chortling twin.

They'd been here for less than a day. They'd changed the castle. Could he walk away?

'She'll love it,' he said softly and the old man followed his gaze.

'She has enough responsibility in looking after the children.' It was almost reproof.

'There are people here who'll help her.'

'Are you saying you want her to take over the administration?'

'There's not that much administration.'

'If you please, Your Highness—'

'Don't call me Your Highness. And he'll gain a crown.' Max was watching Marc duck away from Pippa with a shriek of laughter. 'It's not as if he's getting nothing.'

'No, sir. Marc will gain a crown. The little girls will be princesses. What will your position be? And what will Miss Pippa get?'

Max's gaze swivelled to stare at him. He'd never met this man until tonight. 'You know nothing of this,' he snapped.

'No, sir,' the man agreed. 'I'm only…your valet. And an old friend to your mother. But you do need to make a statement tonight to the castle and to the press. We're suggesting a photo opportunity in the great hall after dinner.'

'A photo opportunity?'

'Mr Levout said we need no such thing,' he said. 'But we

need…the country needs a statement that things are changing.' He motioned to the magnificent clothes. 'We need an official prince.'

'You really want me to dress up?'

'Do you have a choice, sir?'

'Of course I—'

'Do you want the press agreeing with Levout that nothing will change?'

'Dammit… We can't have a photo session without warning Pippa.'

'Shall we make it tomorrow?'

'Three or four days,' he snapped. 'Maybe Thursday.'

'Very well, Your Highness,' the old man said, smiling. 'I'll let the appropriate people know that there'll be an official photograph session on Thursday. But meanwhile I hope you'll wear this uniform tonight, to give Levout the appropriate message.'

'I—'

'He'll be in ceremonial dress,' Blake said smoothly. 'I imagine he'll want to put you on the back step.'

'Dammit…'

'I'll be in your room in an hour to help you dress,' Blake said gently. 'It will be an honour. Your Highness.'

This wasn't right.

She stared at the vast dressing room mirror. Her reflection came back at her from six directions.

Freckles. Coppery curls but short. Snub nose and freckles. Black skirt to her knees. Pink twin-set that had seen better days. Sensible shoes.

Yuk.

She dusted her freckles until they disappeared, stared at herself some more, wiped off too much face powder and saw her freckles emerge again. She grimaced and went into the bedroom.

Beatrice was there. The oldest housemaid. House-matron, Pippa thought. Calling her a housemaid was ridiculous.

She was sitting on the edge of the bed. The kids were curled up under sumptuous covers, waiting to be told a story.

'I should stay,' she said. 'The kids are still awake.'

'We're good,' Sophie said cheerfully. 'Dolores is asleep under the bed and Beattie's going to tell us a story.'

'Just like our grandma did,' Marc added shyly.

'I know a lot of stories,' Beatrice said and smiled at her. 'Go on with you. We know where you are if we need you.'

'In the dining room.'

'The state dining room,' Beatrice corrected her. 'There are six dining rooms.'

'And the state dining room…'

'Is the biggest?'

Pippa took a deep breath. 'Why the biggest? Why tonight?'

'We're all wanting to make a statement to Mr Levout,' she said simply. 'That there's a new royal family in this palace.' She checked Pippa's dress out and her nose wrinkled. 'My dear, have you nothing more…formal?'

'No,' Pippa said bluntly. 'But I'm not actually family. It doesn't matter.'

'No,' Beatrice said doubtfully. 'But the Prince Maxsim—'

'Won't be dressed up,' Pippa said. 'He knows the limitations of my wardrobe. He wouldn't dare.'

She was just a little bit…wrong?

Pippa came down the vast stone staircase, her exploration with the kids holding her in good stead. An ancient butler—the average age of these retainers must be about ninety!—was waiting for her. He swept open the huge double doors into the state dining room. She trod over the threshold and she stopped dead.

Tassles. Sword. Medallions.

Max.

She forgot to breathe.

She'd never seen anything more gorgeous. His Royal Highness, Maxsim de Gautier, Prince Regent of Alp d'Estella.

His suit was jet-black, and it fitted him like a glove. There was a touch of white at his throat and at his wrists, accentuating his tan, the darkness of his eyes and his deep black hair. A vast array of medals and insignia was arranged across his breast. A purple sash slashed across his chest. There were gold tassels on his shoulder—epaulets? There was a braided gold cord on the opposite shoulder to his sash, and another tassel at his hip.

He was wearing a sword.

She had to breathe. She told herself that. Okay, breathe. You can do this.

He took a step towards her and smiled and she forgot to breathe all over again.

'Phillippa…'

It was a couple of moments before she figured out how her voice worked. He was waiting for her to respond. He'd called her Phillippa.

He'd set this up. This formal situation, this amazing dress…

For a girl in a pink twin-set.

'You rat,' she managed at last. 'You bottom-feeding pond scum.'

He blinked. 'Pardon?'

'I'm wearing my church clothes,' she wailed. 'My Sunday best for Tanbarook. What do you think you're doing?'

'Phillippa, here's Mr Levout.'

They weren't alone. For the first time she realised there was another man present—Carver Levout. Like Max, Levout was also in ceremonial regalia. He looked a lot less impressive than Max, but a million times more impressive than Pippa.

One of the buttons had fallen off her cardigan during transit. Pippa had decided since she couldn't find it she'd leave her cardigan open and hope no one would notice. Levout noticed. He stared pointedly at the gap where the button should be, and it was all Pippa could do not to run.

'She's a real provincial,' the man said in his own language to Max, crossing the room to take her hand in his. 'What a drab mouse. Shouldn't we be feeding her in the servants' quarters? She'd be much more comfortable.' He smiled and raised her hand to his lips. 'Charming,' he said in English and then reverted to his own language to add, 'How the hell are we going to cope with her in the public eye? She'll have to be seen as the nanny.'

There was a deathly hush. Levout looked suddenly uncomfortable. Maybe he guessed…

Forget guessing. It was time he knew. 'Then we're four pro-

vincials together,' she said, sweetly in his language. 'Marc and
Sophie and Claire and me. Plus our dog. Provincials all.'

Levout stared. Then he flushed. It was no wonder he'd
assumed she wouldn't speak this language. How many people
did? 'Mademoiselle, I'm devastated,' he started.

'You're also excessively rude. Both of you.'

Max said nothing. He stood in front of the mantel, quietly
watchful.

She ignored him. Or she pretended to ignore him. She'd never
seen a man in a dress sword…

Concentrate on something else, she told herself fiercely. Like
the table. The mahogany table was twelve feet long and it was
so highly polished she could see her face in the wood. There was
a place laid at the head. There were two places set on either side,
halfway down. The cutlery was ornate silverware, each piece a
work of art in its own right. There were, she counted, six crystal
glasses by each plate. An epergne was set in the middle of the
table, silver and gold, all crouching tigers and jungle foliage.

'Goodness,' Pippa said faintly. 'This is amazing. I'm amazed.'
But then she shrugged. She still carefully didn't look at Max but
addressed herself instead to his companion. 'I'm not welcome
here,' she said. 'You've made that clear. You guys can play fancy
dress by yourselves. I'm going to the kitchen to see if I can find
myself a vegemite sandwich.'

'Pippa…' Max said.

'Yeah, I'm Pippa,' she said. 'If you wanted Phillippa you
should have given me warning, but what you see is what you get.
See you later.' She turned and swept out of the room with as much
dignity as a girl in a twin-set with a missing button could muster.

Max caught her before she'd taken half a dozen steps across the
hall. He seized her by her shoulders and turned her to face him.

She was furious. It didn't take a clairvoyant to see that. Her
eyes were bright and wide, and there was a spot of burning
crimson on each cheek.

She turned but she didn't react. She had her arms tightly
folded across her breasts.

'Let me go,' she muttered and she took a step backwards, tugging away.

He released her. 'Pip, I'm sorry.'

'What the hell were you thinking?'

'I don't—'

'There's no need to try and show me up,' she snapped. 'I've never denied I'm a provincial.' She took a deep breath and tilted her chin. 'I'm even proud of it.'

'You're not a provincial.'

'Oh, sure. Max, I'm a child of a single mother. I've scraped a living as best I could. For the last four years I've worked as a navvy on a farm.' She held out her hands, showing work-worn fingers with nails that were cracked and stained. 'I'm illegitimate poor trash and I bet he knows it. I bet you've told him.'

'I haven't. And there's no need to be melodramatic.'

'Says the prince with a dress sword,' she said scornfully. 'I've never seen such a melodramatic outfit in my life.'

'It is, rather,' he said ruefully and stared down at his costume. 'Do you know these pants have fifteen buttons?'

'Fifteen…' Momentarily distracted, she stared at the line of buttons leading from groin to hip. 'Wow.'

'It took me three minutes to do them up,' he said. 'Honest to God.'

She shook her head, dragging her gaze away with difficulty. He was all too good at distracting her. The man was too distracting altogether. 'So you've achieved what?' she demanded, a trifle breathlessly. 'By doing up fifteen buttons?'

'Believe it or not, I've made an old man happy.'

'Levout?'

'There's no way I'll make him happy. He's nervous as hell. What he's just heard has made him even more nervous and what I set in motion in the next few days will give him a palsy stroke. But my valet—'

'Your valet!'

'Ridiculous or not, I have a valet. He's eighty-four. He and the rest of the servants organised this outfit specially and they'd have been desperately hurt if I hadn't worn it tonight. As would the team of people who worked their butts off to get it ready for me. It's amazing.'

'Amazing,' she agreed and tried to turn away again.

He caught her and twisted her back to face him. 'Pippa, you must see how desperate these people are for reassurance. All these people. The royal household and the outside community. This place is a microcosm of the country. We're important.'

'You're important,' she snapped. 'Not me. I'm a provincial.'

'Will you leave it?'

'Not the least bit of warning?' she demanded, still fixated on her missing button. 'No, Pippa, you might want to think about what you're wearing tonight 'cos I'm coming in fancy dress?'

'I thought if I told you what I was wearing you wouldn't come at all. And I didn't know what I was wearing last time I saw you. I'd have had to send a message to the nursery.'

'Or come yourself. It wouldn't be so impossible.'

'I won't come to the nursery.'

'Why not?'

'I don't intend to spend any more time with you than I must.'

Um…maybe that wasn't the wisest thing to say, he thought. He reran the words in his head. Nope, that hadn't sounded good. It had been a really dumb thing to say.

Just because it was true…

The color had drained from Pippa's face. 'What do you mean?' she said at last and he spread his hands.

Okay, maybe it had to be faced. 'Hell, Pippa, you know what I mean. This thing between us…'

'What thing?'

'I shouldn't have kissed you on the plane.'

'No.' She shook her head. 'At least we agree on that.'

'I don't want to give you any ideas.'

Her jaw dropped. 'Of…of all the conceit,' she stammered. 'And so unnecessary. Provincials don't have any ideas. You of all people should know that. After all, you've been mixing with me for days. Of all the arrogant, mean-minded, conceited, over-dressed popinjays—'

'Popinjays?'

'I read it somewhere,' she snapped. 'It's what you are.'

'Levout will be listening to every word.'

'Really?' She raised her voice.

'Look, it was your idea that I stay here. Not mine.'

'Don't you dare do this to me.'

'Dare do what?'

'Take my concern for the children as some sort of interest in you. I don't want you here. Your presence, however, guarantees security for Marc and Sophie and Claire. You go, then we go. But you're right. We needn't spend any more time together than we must. Not because I just might jump you, Maxsim de Gautier, but because I might slap your handsome, arrogant face.'

'You wouldn't,' he said.

And once again he knew he'd said the wrong thing.

She'd never hit anyone in her life. She'd never dreamed of doing it. But now, as they stood in this gilded hallway full of ancient, over-the-top artwork, chandeliers, servants in the doorways, Levout standing open-mouthed behind them, the emotions of the last few days found irresistible expression.

As a slap it was a beauty. It was straight across his cheek. The sound of the slap was louder than the voice she was using.

She backed off and stared at him. What little vestige of color she'd had before was completely gone now.

'Pippa…' he said, uncertainly, and she raised her hands to her face as if her head needed support. As if it were she who'd been slapped.

'I-I'm so sorry,' she stammered, aghast.

'You don't—'

'I'd never slap. I never would. It's just…'

'We've hauled you right out of your comfort zone.'

'I don't have a comfort zone,' she whispered. 'The farm? Taking care of the kids by myself? That's not comfort. What I use as a comfort zone is independence. I don't need anyone. I don't need you. And for you to assume that just because you kissed me I'd see you as some kind of love interest…'

'I never assumed that.'

'Yes, you did,' she said steadying a little. 'And maybe you're right. Maybe I have been a bit too attracted to you. But now...' She shrugged. 'Well, I've been told and I'm not stupid, regardless of what you think. We're here for a month while I figure out whether the kids could have a future here. You're my...bond, if you like. My surety. I'm demanding that you stay here too. But only until I figure out whether we're safe. If that's tomorrow then you can take yourself back to Paris.'

He hesitated. He should finish this. But there were imperatives. 'Pippa, the press...'

'What about the press?'

'They want to see you again.'

'Not me.'

'They want to see the children. They need a photo opportunity.'

'Then we'll set one up. Let Beatrice know and I'll make sure they have clean faces.'

'They want to meet you. Tonight if possible.'

'No deal.' She backed again so she was at the foot of the stairs. 'Now is there anything else?'

'Then Thursday. For an official portrait? We have to let the press see us.'

'Thursday,' she snapped. 'Fine. I'll sew on my button for the occasion. Make sure it's at night 'cos twin-set and skirt looks dumb in this heat.'

'Dinner is served,' the butler intoned from behind them and Max winced.

'Can we delay it for a little?'

'No,' Pippa said and squared her shoulders. 'We're all hungry but we're not eating together.' She walked over to the tray the butler was carrying—three bowls of soup. She lifted one and smelled. 'Yum. Asparagus. My favourite. I'll take mine out on the terrace.'

'You can't,' Max said blankly.

'Watch me. Or don't watch me. In fact I forbid you to watch me. You and Mr Levout go back to your dress-ups. This provincial's going to eat her meal outside. That way I can burp and slurp just the way I like.'

'That's ridiculous.'

'I'm not ridiculous,' she snapped. 'You're the one with the sword.'

CHAPTER SEVEN

PIPPA might be in a fairy tale, but three days later she was starting to be just a bit...bored? When they were on holidays on the farm the kids played happily independently. Here she stuck with them like glue, but after three days she was wondering if it was more to protect herself than to protect the kids.

Carver still gave her the creeps, but it was Max she was avoiding. Max and his wonderful uniform. How dared a man look so sexy?

All the staff were treating him as if it were Max who was the Crown Prince.

They weren't treating him as if he was an illegitimate outsider. She was uneasy, puzzled, and increasingly she was restless.

'The last two princes spent very little time at the castle,' Beatrice told her. 'The casinos at Monte Carlo were more their style, and our rulers encouraged them.'

'Your rulers?'

'We have a President and a Council. Mr Levout is on the Council. They run this country.'

'Why haven't we met this President?'

'I suspect he's desperately trying to work out how these children can be blocked from the throne. If he can, there's no one else in direct succession and the Principality will disappear. That would leave the Levout family in control.'

'Max doesn't want that.'

'And thank God for Max,' Beatrice told her. 'He is a wonderful prince, and he seems to be a good man.'

There it was again, the blank acceptance of an outsider as a prince.

'Yeah, but not necessarily a nice one,' she managed, and Beatrice regarded her with the beginning of a tiny smile.

'I don't know about that,' she said. 'Maybe we'll wait and see.'

So she waited. But by the fourth day she was openly admitting she was climbing walls.

How could she be bored in a place like this? she wondered. There was as much wonderful food as she and the children needed. There was no need to milk a hundred and twenty cows twice a day. In fact, the dairyman had refused her offer to help. 'It wouldn't be proper,' he told her and he refused to budge. There were swimming pools and wonderful gardens. There were gentle people waiting on her every whim, even eager for her to have whims.

For Pippa, who'd worked hard every day of her adult life, it felt wrong. Max wasn't used to this either, she thought, and she wondered how he was taking it. She wasn't asking him, though. Whenever she saw him she'd head for the nearest child.

She was being a coward, she knew, but he seriously unsettled her, and life was strange enough without being…unsettled.

'Let's leave this relationship businesslike,' she told him when he confronted her. 'If there's something you need then of course we'll talk, but the castle staff got the wrong idea when I slapped you and there's no way we want to encourage that.'

'The wrong idea? That I've brought back with me a termagant?'

'I don't know what a termagant is,' she said huffily. 'And I've got far too many good manners to ask.'

She waited for him to respond. He didn't, though. He stood and gazed at her for a long moment and then turned away.

Good.

But increasingly their disassociation seemed ever so slightly silly. And she had to admit that she missed him. She looked up termagant in the dictionary and huffed in indignation—but it was a bit lonely to huff by yourself.

'You've been by yourself for years,' she scolded herself, but it didn't work.

She'd sort of got used to Max.

But the avoidance seemed to be working both ways, and a girl had some pride.

On the fourth day she finished breakfast, looked at the day stretching out in front of her and decided on a walk. 'Right round the castle grounds,' she told the kids and they groaned.

'But Beattie's grandkids are coming,' Marc said. 'Beattie says Sally's the same age as me and Rodrick's the same age as Sophie and Claire. Aimee's bigger than everyone but Beatrice said she knows skipping games.'

'They'll be fine with me,' Beatrice told her. She'd been making their bed—Pippa wasn't even permitted to do that. 'I promise I'll keep them with me all the time. Why don't you go for a walk by yourself?'

Because I'm scared of meeting Max, she thought, but that was a dumb reason. She couldn't voice it. She looked helplessly across at Beatrice and Beatrice smiled.

'He's not an ogre, dear,' she said gently. 'Blake says he's a sweetheart. He says he takes after his lovely mother. Bless him.'

Oh, great. Yeah, he's a sweetheart and that's the whole problem, she thought, but she couldn't say that either.

Right. A walk. She gave herself a firm talking-to, which consisted of standing in front of her six-dimensional mirror and talking severely to all six of her. Then she waved goodbye to her various images and went to find Dolores.

But Dolores wasn't interested either. Sixteen was really old for such a big dog, and she'd suffered badly this winter. Here she moved from fire to sunbeam and back again, soaking up the warmth with the same intensity she'd once reserved for rabbits. She was stretched out now on the patio, soaking in sun, and as Pippa bent to pat her she barely raised the energy to wag her tail. As Pippa stroked her she gave a long, slow shudder of pure, unadulterated bliss.

'At least I've done the right thing by you, girl,' Pippa whispered, blinking hard. She knew Dolores didn't have long. To give her another summer…

She'd done something right.

But she missed her dog by her side. She now had no kids, no work, no dog. The sensation as she took herself off for a walk was strangely empty.

'Other people have holidays,' she told herself. 'Get over it.'

But she couldn't. What she saw stretching out before her was strange—a life here as the children's guardian. A life that wasn't her life.

A life even without Dolores?

'Oh, forget it with the maudlin,' she told herself. 'Walk.'

She walked. It was a long way around the castle grounds—too far to walk in a morning. She walked for an hour, around a vast lake, through woods where she startled deer, into the hills behind the castle, but she still wasn't halfway round. Finally she gave up on the perimeter and veered cross country.

The woods here were so dense they were almost scary, but there was hammering and shouting and sounds of construction in the distance. Where there was construction there was civilisation, so she pushed her way through overgrown paths to find it.

It *was* a construction site. It was a small cottage, with what looked like an extension being built at the back.

Max was up on the roof. He was wearing faded jeans and a heavy cotton workman's shirt, open at the throat and with sleeves rolled up to the elbows. He was fitting roofing slates. The sun was glinting on his dark hair. He was laughing at something someone below had just said.

He looked...

Whoa.

She would have backed away—fast—but he saw her. His hands stilled. The slate in his hand was set down with care.

'Pippa,' he said and the pleasure in his voice gave her a completely inappropriate wash of warmth. Maybe he'd found the last four days as long as she had.

He didn't look bored, she thought with a pang of jealousy. He looked...

Whoa again.

'Hi,' she managed, trying to keep her voice in order. 'I've been walking.'

'Hiking, more like. You're miles from home. Did you bring a packed lunch?'

'No, I—'

'You're bored?'

'No,' she lied, looking about her. There were three other men on the site, elderly men—of course—working on a pile of bricks.

'They don't need help at the dairy?' Max asked.

'They say it's not seemly.' She glowered. 'How come it's seemly for you to fix roofs but not for me to milk cows?'

He grinned. 'Desperate times lead to desperate measures. Sleeping by the pool is great for an hour but I get itchy fingers. You want to clean some bricks? Is your back up to it?'

'My back's fine. Why are you cleaning bricks?'

'This house is for Blake and Beatrice.' He motioned to one of the elderly men who raised his cap in a deferential greeting. 'You've met Blake? He and Beatrice lived here for over forty years. But five years ago there was a storm and the back section collapsed. See that pile of bricks over there?' She looked to where he was pointing. 'That's the remains of the fireplace. Anyway Blake and Beatrice moved into the servant's quarters in the palace but the servant's quarters needs a bomb. It'll take time and patience to get it brought up to scratch. Meanwhile I thought we could rebuild.'

We. She looked cautiously around her, recognising the butler, the valet, and one of the footmen. Average again about ninety.

'Right,' she said.

'The boys are chipping old mortar off the bricks. Want to help?' And he smiled.

Damn him, why did he do that? He just had to let those dark eyes twinkle and she was lost.

She should go.

But this was a real job. She ached for a job. Of the three geriatrics, one was holding the ladder in case Max ever came down. The other two were chipping gamely at old mortar.

She watched them work for a minute. At this rate they'd be lucky if they had the bricks cleaned by the end of the millennium.

But why was Max here? 'I thought you said there were lots of administration things that needed doing.'

'Not until the succession's in place. The lawyers are working on it.' He picked up his slate with purpose. 'Meanwhile are you going to help or are you going to stand there distracting me?'

'I'm not distracting you.'

'Little you know,' Max growled. 'Give the lady a pair of gloves, Blake, and let's get this moving.'

He sat on the roof replacing tile after tile, his hands moving methodically but his mind all on the lady beneath him.

She was amazing. She was cleaning at a rate more than double that of the old men, but she chattered to the men as she worked, distracting them just as much as she was distracting him, but for a purpose. As she cleaned she slipped her finished bricks into one of three piles, so the piles in front of her companions were growing at the same rate as hers. Giving them back their pride.

The men were enjoying her. They worked together, they paused and laughed and wiped their brows and they stopped for a drink, but she methodically worked on. Jean, the footman who'd been holding the ladder, decided it didn't really need holding and went over to help.

Well, why wouldn't he? She was…magnetic.

And she was surely used to hard work. The bricks were hard to clean but they were flying through her hands. At the thought of what she'd been facing for the last four years his gut clenched.

So he'd solved that problem. He'd brought her here.

But she'd never be seen on the same pegging as the children, he thought. Levout was making that perfectly clear. She was a provincial, no blood relative of the heir to the throne, and with no delineated role as his was.

Maybe she'd leave.

No. She'd never leave the children.

But what would her position be?

They stopped for half an hour at lunch time and Max used his cell-phone to check the children.

'Our visitors are staying for lunch,' Beatrice said happily. 'And then they'll all need a nap. Tell Pippa to come home if she wants to, but there's no need.'

Max relayed the message and saw confusion wash across her face.

'They still need you,' he said gently.

'Of course.'

'Have a sandwich.'

'Thank you,' she said, and took a huge cheese sandwich from the pile, biting into it like a man.

He grinned.

'What?' she demanded.

'Nothing.'

'Yeah, and I wipe my mouth on my sleeve too,' she said darkly. 'Butt out, Your Highness.'

'Of course.'

The men had brought beer. 'We'll send to the house to get something more suitable,' Blake told him. He seemed distressed that Max and Pippa were sharing their plain luncheon. Pippa shook her head and lifted a bottle.

'Hey, we're not proper royalty,' she said. 'We're just hangers on. This is wet and it's cold and if anyone tries taking this from me I'll spray them with it.'

'You are royalty,' Blake said, eyeing Max with reproof, but Max ignored him. Finally the men chuckled and relaxed. Gentle banter continued as they sat under a huge oak and surveyed their hard work.

Max hardly participated in the banter. He leaned back and listened to Pippa laughing with the men, joking with them, teasing with them.

Her jeans and her T-shirt were coated in brick-dust. There was dust in her curls and a streak down her cheek where dust had mixed with sweat. She'd scraped her arm and there was a trickle of dried blood to her wrist. She was laughing at something one of the men was saying, and she was drinking beer straight from the bottle.

She was the loveliest thing he'd ever seen.

Yeah, right, and where was that going to get him? Into disaster?

He couldn't go there even if he wanted to, he thought. How the hell would his mother react? I've fallen in love with the guardian of the new Crown Prince. I have to stay in Alp d'Estella.

She'd break her heart. After all that had been done to her… After all she'd done to herself… How could he ask it of her?

He looked up and saw Pippa watching him.

'It looks grim,' she said.

'What?'

'What you're thinking.'

'I was thinking about slates.'

'Really?' she said and hiked her eyebrows.

Their telepathy wasn't a one-way thing, he thought, and h
turned away, ostensibly to pack up the lunch gear but in reality s
she couldn't see his face any more. He had to get this under contro

It was bad enough that he was here now, and his mother knew
he was here. After the official photo shoot she'd see him in ever
glossy magazine in Europe.

He grabbed a handful of slates and carted them up onto th
roof. No one saw him go—even Jean, his ladder holder, wa
chuckling over something Pippa had just said, hanging onto ever
word. Good, he thought. It was good that they were falling in lov
with her. It was great for the people. It was great for the country

But what would her position be?

It had to be made formal, he thought, or she'd be shunted int
the background for ever. Which meant that he had to drag he
into this photo shoot, whether she liked it or not.

'Pippa, we're giving a press conference this evening,' he calle
from the safety of his roof, and she stared up at him.

'How did you get up there?'

'I climbed.'

'No one held your ladder. Those slates are heavy.'

'I'm fine. Jean has better things to do than hold my ladde
But about this shoot.'

'Shoot?'

'Photo shoot. Introduction to your new royal family.'

'I'll dress the kids up.'

'Beatrice is sorting something for them,' he called. 'There
actually traditional costume for royal children.'

'It's very splendid,' Jean, the footman, told her gravely. 'An
colourful. The girls' dresses have fourteen petticoats.'

'And the boy's costume is just as colourful,' Blake added. '
had petticoats too, but the last prince put his foot down aged a
of four so we converted it to trousers. It has what looks like
small apron over the front but it's unexceptional and mos

children are envious when they see it. Beatrice measured the children the first night you were here and the costumes are ready.'

'Well, that's sorted,' Pippa said, and went back to brick-cleaning. She looked perturbed, though, Max thought. Worrying that things were being taken from her control. As indeed they could be if she wasn't included.

'We'd like you to dress up too,' he called, and Pippa paused mid-brick.

'Me.'

'Yes.'

'I'm not royal.' She made a recovery and waved a brick in his direction. 'Do I look royal?'

'Yes, miss,' Blake said severely, answering before Max could get a word in. 'We believe you look extremely royal. Don't we, Jean? Don't we, Pascal-Marie? Almost as royal as His Highness, Prince Maxsim.'

'Yes,' his companions agreed gravely.

'Then I'll come to the shoot wearing what I've got on,' she said and grinned and started chipping again.

'You can't,' Max called. 'This is important, Pippa. These photographs will be in every major glossy worldwide.'

She paused, mid-chop. 'Even in Tanbarook?'

'I'm guessing even in Tanbarook. Aussie girl becomes a European princess...'

'I'm guardian of a prince. That doesn't make me a princess.'

No. It didn't. That was the problem, he thought. There was only one way she could become a princess—and there was no way he was going down that route.

But she had to have a formal role. She was the children's guardian. She had to be in the shoot if she was to retain any sort of authority when he left.

'Miss, the castle can't be left with just three royal children,' Blake told her, echoing Max's thoughts.

'Levout will take charge again,' Pascal-Marie—the butler—added. 'Levout's like a bear with a sore head now that Prince Maxsim is here. But Prince Maxsim intends to leave at the end of one month.'

'We might too,' Pippa said and the old men's faces fell.

'No.'

'Possibly not,' she whispered.

'Then you need to have a role here,' Max called. 'My deputy or something similar. The people have to know you. You need to be part of the press conference.'

'In my twin-set? I still haven't found the button.'

'Beatrice could organise you something,' Blake said, but he sounded doubtful. 'Maybe her ideas are a little old-fashioned…'

'No,' Max said, shoving a slate into place and concentrating on the next one. 'There's a reasonable shopping centre in the village. I'll finish here in an hour and take you.'

'I've no money for clothes.'

'You're the guardian of the heir to the throne of Alp d'Estella. You should have been getting a suitable allowance long since. You are now. Get used to it.'

She didn't want to go to town with him.

Pippa chipped on, seemingly concentrating only on her bricks but in reality twisting the forthcoming journey into all sorts of threatening contortions.

It was only shopping, she thought, but she'd be alone with Max and she didn't want to be alone with Max.

She could take the children.

Right, and they'd be so good while she chose a frock. Ha. Shopping with them was a nightmare at the best of times.

Who else could she take?

No one without saying straight out that she didn't trust Max, and it wasn't actually that she didn't trust Max. She didn't trust herself.

She worked steadily on, trying to get her head together, trying to stay calm.

An hour later Max came up behind her, took the brick from her fingers and she jumped about a foot.

'Enough.'

'I haven't done enough,' she said, suddenly breathless, and the men around her laughed.

'You've put the rest of us to shame, miss,' Blake said. 'You deserve a rest. Have fun.'

'Let's go,' Max said and lifted her chisel from her hand. 'Work's over for the day.'

'I won't be able to leave the kids. I've been away from them all day.'

'Let's check, shall we?' he said. 'Make no assumptions, scary or otherwise.'

'Why would they be scary?'

'We both know the answer to that,' he said softly. 'Though neither of us know what to do with it.'

Was he saying he was as attracted to her as she was to him? Pippa sat in the passenger seat of a neat little sports car and tried to concentrate on the scenery, but it was impossible to concentrate on something other than the man beside her.

Was he saying the avoidance of the last four days had been part of his plan as well as hers?

Good, she thought. Great. If they both thought this relationship was impossible then they could do something about it. Or do nothing, which would be a much more suitable plan.

She was sitting as far apart as she could, which was a start—though you couldn't get very far apart in a tiny sports car.

'Does this car belong to the palace?'

'It's mine. Do you like it?'

'I do,' she said politely. The little car practically purred as they negotiated the scenic curves around the mountains. 'Actually it's smashing,' she admitted. 'The kids would love it.'

'Just lucky they were too busy to come, then.'

They had been too busy. When Pippa had gone to find them they had been in the vegetable garden, sorting worms from loamy compost. Dolores had been nearby, sleeping in the sun and keeping a benign eye on her charges.

'We're making a carrot bed,' the twins told Pippa. 'We need worms. M. Renagae says there can never be enough worms in a carrot bed.'

They were fitting into this life to the manor born, Pippa

thought. It was only Pippa who felt…foreign. She'd asked—use-lessly—whether they'd like to go into town to shop and they'd regarded her as if she were a sandwich short of a picnic.

So now she was alone with Max, and he was staring ahead as if he was as determined as she was not to cross the line.

'What sort of dress do I need?' she asked.

'Several. A long gown for the formal photo and a couple more for dinners.'

'I eat with the children.'

'I hope after I leave that you'll stand in my stead on State occasions.'

'You're assuming I'm staying.'

'I'm assuming you're thinking about it. This place has to be better than where I found you.'

'It might be,' she said, still cautious. 'Max, what are you afraid of?'

'I'm not afraid.'

'Then what? What aren't you telling me?'

'Nothing.'

'Don't lie to me,' she snapped. 'I know there's something. It's just intuition but I know there's…something.' She hesitated, but it had to be said—what she'd been thinking these last four days. 'It's not just the castle. It's royalty itself, so much so that you're scared of even being with me.'

'I'm shopping with you now, aren't I?'

'Only because you're trying to persuade me to take the next step—whatever that is. For the last four days you've been avoiding me as much as I've been avoiding you. Why? Because you're scared you might get attached to me and to the kids? Or is it that you're scared you might be called into account for what you've done?'

'Your imagination's acting overtime,' he said grimly.

'I know it is. But all I have is my imagination as I don't have facts.'

'You don't need—'

'Don't you dare tell me what I need or don't need,' she flashed, swivelling in the car to face him. 'You've talked me into coming

here with your promise of warmth and luxury and relief from responsibility, but the responsibility's followed me and I'm damned
if I'm letting your charm and good looks and…your princeliness
deflect me from figuring out what I have to figure. Just because
you wear a stupid dress sword—'

'Princeliness?'

'Don't laugh at me.'

'I wouldn't.'

'You would if you thought it would help. But I still get the
feeling you're afraid. If not of me—and that's crazy—if not of
emotion, then what?'

'Nothing.'

'Stop the car.'

'I can't. There's only two hours before the shops close.'

'Then talk fast,' she snapped, suddenly sure of herself. There
was something. If not fear, then what? She was responsible for
Marc. She had to find out. 'Please stop the car,' she repeated. 'I'm
taking not one minute's more part in this charade before I know
what I need to know.'

He stopped in a pullover catering for tourists who wanted to
gaze down the valley at the winding river and the spectacular
mountains beyond. The scenery was awesome, but Max gazed
straight ahead and saw nothing. 'What do you want to know?'
he said blankly.

'About your family, for a start,' she said. She wasn't sure
where she was going with this. She wasn't even sure that she
wasn't a bit crazy. She stared down at her hands, which were
suddenly the most interesting things she could find to look at—
apart from Max and there was no way she was looking at him any
more. 'I want to know about Thiérry. Tell me about the car crash.'

'Thiérry died in a car crash when he was seventeen.' He said
it as if goaded.

She flashed a look at him then, just for a moment, and then
looked back at her hands. 'With your father. Who was drunk?'

'Of course with my father,' he exploded. 'Of course he was
drunk. He's a de Gautier. The blood's cursed.'

'Ooh, who's being melodramatic?' she whispered and he stared at her in astonishment.

'You're accusing me of melodrama?'

'If you're talking about cursed blood, then, yes, I am,' she said with asperity. 'Tell it like it is, Max. Don't try and make my blood curdle. I'm a nurse, remember? It takes a whole lot more than curses to curdle my blood.'

'I guess it would.'

She looked at him for a long moment, gave a tiny smile and a decisive nod.

'That's better. Now start again. Your…father was responsible for Thiérry's death? How did it happen?'

He sighed. 'Okay. The whole story. Not that it helps anything.'

'I'm listening.'

'My father…' He sighed again. 'Apparently there's been contention and hatred in the royal family for generations. My father was raised thinking he was owed a birthright, that he had a claim on the throne, or at least part of its wealth, but the way the succession's written he got nothing. He spent much of his time here, freeloading on the old prince. He married my mother which was the only sane thing he did in his life, but the marriage didn't last. She was seventeen and besotted with royalty, and he met and married her on a whim. By the time she had Thiérry she knew it was a disaster.'

'And she couldn't…leave?'

'Are you kidding? My father was seeing Thiérry as a potential heir to the throne. The old Crown Prince Paul was an invalid. There was only Bernard, and Bernard was…effete. There's clauses written into most royal marriages, and ours is no exception. If the marriage ends then any children stay under the sole care of the sovereign.'

He paused, his eyes bleak and cold and distant. Pippa didn't say anything. She couldn't think of anything to say.

'So my mother had an affair,' he said at last. 'Desperation? Who can blame her? She became pregnant with me, and the old prince kicked her out of the castle. He was so angry that he kicked them all out—my father and Thiérry included.'

'So then…'

'My father was furious, of course, and humiliated, but he was back to living on his wits, and he didn't want a baby. So he turned his back on all of us. Mama was permitted to return to her parents' farm, taking Thiérry with her. We saw no more of the royal family. Only then the old prince died. Bernard became Crown Prince but still hadn't married, so Thiérry was his heir and my father appeared on the scene again. Thiérry was seventeen—a rebellious teenager hating the poverty we were living in—and my father was demanding to show him his heritage.'

'But not you,' she whispered. 'Where do you fit in?'

'I don't. I was the product of an affair. I was worthless.'

She swallowed. But then she thought of the things that weren't making sense. Blake's insistence on Max's royalty. The servants' insistence. They'd all been in the castle then…

They'd have known. There was something in the way they deferred to Max, as if he were the Crown Prince.

'You were really his son,' she whispered, knowing suddenly that it had to be true, and he didn't deny it.

'Yes,' he said at last. 'But I've only known myself for a few weeks. I was approached to take on the regency. I refused and finally my mother told me who I really was. She'd never spoken of it. I know it now, and, for some reason I can't figure, Blake knows it. But as far as I know, no one else. She lied because she couldn't bear to live here, and by lying about my parentage at least she'd still have me.'

'Oh, Max…'

'So there you have it,' he said bleakly. 'The makings of tragedy, from which I, as a supposed bastard, was excluded. My father, in his expensive car, in his amazing royal regalia, must have seemed like something out of a fairy story to seventeen-year-old Thiérry. But my mother was appalled. I still remember the shouting. The tears. Finally Mama agreed that Thiérry could visit the castle, but she insisted on accompanying him.'

'Of course.'

'You know, my mother would love you,' he said dryly. 'You

sound just like her—a mother hen ready to take on all comers.'
He smiled but she didn't smile back

'So what happened?'

'Boring really. Predictably horrible. He loaded them into his
too-fast car, he drove erratically—probably shouting at my
mother all the time—and they all came off one of the cliffs somewhere close to here. My father and Thiérry were killed instantly.
My mother's now a paraplegic.'

Pippa had stopped looking at her hands. Instead she was
staring down at the river, looping lazily round the base of the
cliffs below.

'Oh, Max,' she said at last. 'Oh, poor lady.'

'Mama knows as I do that someone has to accept the Crown if
the people aren't to face ruin. But she won't go back on what she's
said. That I was the result of an affair. That I have no connection
to the palace. The fact that I look like a damned de Gautier…'

'There's DNA testing.'

'So there is. If I wanted to prove it.'

'But you don't?'

'I won't do it to her. For why? To take a throne I don't want?
If I can organise things without it…if I can set up the regency…'
He sighed. 'You do what you have to do.'

'Of course.' She linked her fingers again, but her gaze was still
on the river. The trap was closing in on her, she thought dully
as it had closed on Max. It might be a gilded cage, but it was a
cage for all that. 'You know what I'd really like?' she whispered.

'What?'

'To go back to nursing.'

'Nursing!'

'Don't say it like it's a bad smell,' she snapped, and suddenly
she was furious. Here she was again, in the middle of a mess,
expected to pick up the pieces with no complaint. Well, she
might, but, dammit, he was going to understand that she was
giving up something too. 'If you knew how hard I worked to get
my nursing qualifications… Every summer I've worked my
fingers to the bone to get enough money to keep me at school.
That started from the time I was ten, working illegally peeling

potatoes for our local fish and chip shop. But somehow I did it. I finally qualified as a nurse and I loved it. Independence! You can't imagine. I kept right on studying. I wanted to be the best nurse in the world, but you know what? Life just got in the way.'

'Life as in Marc and Claire and Sophie.'

'And you,' she said bitterly. She glared at him. 'Oh, there's no use complaining. But don't you dare look at me now and say there's a really luxurious castle and you'll be waited on hand and foot so what else can you possibly want from life? I bet that's what your father told your mother. So here I am. I don't even have a definite role. I'm not royal. I can't help in the running of this country. I'm going to have to put up with people like Levout patronising me until Marc is twenty-one and I can get on with my own life. Whatever that is. I don't think I have one,' she said. 'You sure as hell don't think I do.'

'Pippa…'

'Start the car,' she said wearily. 'Yes, you're in a bind, but I am too. I need to think. Meanwhile there's no need to be nice to me any more. I know what you want now and I need to decide on my own terms. Let's find this dress.'

'I'm sorry.'

'No, you're not. You're on track to get out of here. Start the car.'

'If I could—'

'Yeah, and if I could,' she retorted. 'But we can't. We're stuck in this royal groove and you have three and a half weeks of it left and I'm looking at thirteen years. Let's go.'

'I don't feel I can.'

She sighed. 'Of course you can,' she said. 'Like me, you have no choice. I agree, your mother's given you no choice. I bet if I met her I'd agree with your decision entirely. I'm sorry I flung that at you. It served no purpose.'

'Except to make me see what I should have seen last week.'

'There's no point.' She took a deep breath. 'Max, it was dumb for me to say that. It was just…anger, and anger achieves nothing. I don't usually let fly. It won't happen again.'

'I hate this.'

'That makes two of us.'

He stared at her for a long minute, and then raised his hand to her face and cupped the curve of her cheek. She let his hand rest there for a moment, allowing herself the luxury of taking warmth and strength that she so desperately needed. But she couldn't depend on it.

She was alone. She knew it. She'd been alone in Tanbarook and she was alone here. The future stretched out before her, bleak and endless.

Bleak? Hey, she was going to live in a castle. 'Don't *you* start being melodramatic,' she said out loud and Max frowned.

'Pardon?'

'I was talking to me.' She lifted his hand away, but she didn't quite release it.

'You're a wonderful woman.'

'I am, aren't I?' she said and she summoned a smile. 'But I need a dress.'

'Sure you do.' But he was gazing at her with such a look...

'Don't you dare kiss me,' she muttered and hauled her hand away.

'Why not?'

'You know very well why not. You and me? No and no and no. We're in enough of a dilemma. A casual affair would mess things between us for ever.'

'I'm not talking about a casual—'

'You're not talking about anything. Take me shopping, Max.' She twisted so she was staring straight ahead and her fingers started knotting again. 'What are we waiting for?'

'I don't have a clue,' Max said slowly. He stared at her for a long moment, but she didn't look at him. Conversation ended.

Finally he turned the key in the ignition and steered his car out of the pullover and around the cliffs into town.

CHAPTER EIGHT

THE village might be tiny, but it catered for money.

'Monaco's within easy driving distance and we have amazing summers,' Max said. He was playing tourist guide, his smooth, informative chat proving the safest of conversations. 'So we have Europe's wealthy summering here, driving between here and the casinos.' He pulled into a parking lot in front of a dozen quaint shops. 'Daniella's your best choice. The dress shop on the corner.'

'You'd know that, how?'

'Beatrice told me,' he said, looking wounded.

Pippa even managed a laugh. 'Okay. Daniella's it is. How much do I have to spend?'

'As much as you like.' He climbed out of the car and came round to open her door. 'The royal fortune is entailed. That means it's been kept safe and there's more than enough to pay for you to wear what you like. Diamond-studded knickers if that's what takes your fancy.'

She choked. 'It doesn't.'

'How did I know you'd say that?' He grinned. 'Let's go.'

'You're not shopping with me.' She was too close to him, she thought. Damn him for his good manners. She wanted him back on the other side of the car.

'Of course I'm coming.'

'Of course nothing. I'm having no man saying, "Nope, that's not suitable," or "That color makes you look consumptive," or, "Gee, I like that one, it gives you great bazookers."'

'Bazookers?'

'See, you don't even know the language. How do I pay?'

He hesitated, but her chin was tilting in a gesture he was starting to know.

'Fine,' he said, conceding defeat. Maybe she was right. They needed to keep their distance. He produced an embossed card. 'You need a couple of dinner dresses, one over-the-top evening dress and anything else that catches your eye. I'll be drinking coffee in Vlados, over the road.'

'Fine,' she repeated, and looked at the card. 'You sure this'll work?'

'I'm sure. Daniella will recognise it. She'll probably have heard about you. She'll certainly have heard about the children. Pippa…'

'Yes?'

She was standing in the late-afternoon sunshine, chin tilted, dredging up courage. David against Goliath.

It was important to maintain distance.

He couldn't. It was too much for any man. It was too much for him.

'Good luck in your hunting,' he said softly. His fingers caught her under the chin and tilted her chin just a tiny bit more. He kissed her. Softly, fleetingly, withdrawing before she had time to react.

'Go to it, my David,' he told her and he smiled and turned away to find his coffee shop.

Max bought a newspaper. He settled in at Vlados and ordered a coffee. He drank half a cup; there was a commotion in the entrance and there was Pippa.

She was in the midst of a group of uniformed men. Subdued. In her simple jeans and her T-shirt and sandals, she looked absurdly defenseless. David defeated?

He was on his feet and moving towards her before she saw him. 'Pippa?'

She turned, relief washing over her face. She broke away from the men and met him halfway across the restaurant. She was not only defeated, he thought. She was furious. Her eyes were sparking daggers and spots of high colour suffused each cheek.

She tossed down the card on the nearest table. With force. 'Great idea, Your Highness.'

'What?'

'I don't look royal.'

'You look pretty good to me,' he said and smiled, and then he stopped smiling as she looked around as if she was searching for something to brain him with. 'Hey, I'm not the bad guy here. At least,' he said cautiously, 'I don't think I am.'

'You're not,' she said, glaring at the group of men she'd just left. 'But you gave me the stupid card.'

'The card was a problem?'

'The whole idea was a problem.'

'Are you going to t—'

It seemed she was going to tell. 'I'd barely set foot over the threshold,' she told him. 'Before Daniella herself—all coiffure and glitter—came snaking out from behind the counter and wondered if I was in the right shop. I said I needed three formal dresses and if she had formal dresses then I was in the right shop.'

He was baffled. She looked really close to tears, he thought. He badly wanted to hold her but if he did…she'd back off, he thought, and he made a huge effort to make his voice noncommittal. 'So?'

'So she became very formal. She showed me a dress which looked okay, even if it did look like it was at the bottom of the range she carried. I said could I try it and she said, for security, could she see some form of identification as well as my credit card. I was getting pretty peeved, but I need a damned dress so I gave her my passport and your dumb royal card.'

'I see,' he said, really cautiously. He didn't see.

'So instead of helping me change into the dress she showed me into a cubicle. Then while I was wrangling zips she rang Levout. Who said I had no authority to charge anything to the castle and I must have stolen the card and he'd send the police straight away.'

'You are kidding,' he said slowly, but he knew already that she wasn't. Uh-oh.

'So I came out of the change room looking the ants pants in a little black number that would have knocked your socks off and I was met by six policemen. Six! And they wanted to haul me away in all my finery. Only then Daniella set up a screech about her dress, which she said costs a fortune, which, by the way, I was never going to buy because it was scratchy, and she made me take it off. Then and there. She made me change without going into the cubicle. She told the men to face the street but she wouldn't let me go back into the change room. She watched every step of the way in case I hurt her precious frock. I was humiliated to my socks and she watched me change like I was a criminal and even though I was wearing the most respectable knickers in the world all the time I was getting so…so…'

Hell. His hands were clenched into his palms so hard they hurt.

'Anyway, I got back in my own gear,' she muttered, as if she was trying hard to move on. 'Then the police said I was under arrest, and I saw red. I said I hadn't stolen your stupid card and that you were here and you'd sent me to buy a dress and you're in charge of their stupid police force and you'll sack the lot of them and if they didn't check with you first you'll have their necks on the guillotine first thing in the morning.'

'Hey,' he said, almost startled out of anger. 'Guillotine?'

'Well, maybe I didn't say quite that,' she muttered, glowering. 'But it's what I meant. Daniella's horrible coiffure would look great in a bucket, and I'd knit and watch like anything. Anyway, then they thought they'd check with you. So they frogmarched me over here—well, why wouldn't they when Levout assured them I was nothing to do with you? Now they've seen you and they're really nervous. But they're waiting on your command right now, to take me out and shoot me at dawn.'

There were six burly police officers in the doorway, muttering fiercely among themselves. Looking uncomfortable. As well they might.

'They seem to know you,' she said, anger becoming calmer now. 'Not me, though. I'm a provincial.'

'I'll go talk to them.'

'Good. I'll go steal a beer from the bar.'

'Maybe a coffee would be better. Vlados will fetch one for you.'

'Why not live up to my reputation?'

'Pippa?'

'Yes.'

'Have a coffee.'

By the time he reached them, the policemen were pretty sure they were in the wrong. Pippa's anger must have been obvious, as was the conciliatory hand Max put on her shoulder as he left her.

'Did she have rights to use the card?' the officer with the most stripes asked before he said a word.

'Yes,' Max said, dangerously calm. 'You saw our photographs taken the day we arrived? Did you recognise her?'

'Yes, but she isn't royal. We're sorry if we've made a mistake, though. We were acting on Levout's orders.'

'You have made a mistake. And what possible authority does Levout have over you?'

'He assured us the card was stolen.'

'You haven't answered my question. Was it his suggestion that made you force Miss Donohue to strip in the centre of the shop?'

'I…no. That was Miss Daniella's idea. She was concerned about her clothing.'

'And you agreed? You stood by while someone was forced to strip in public?'

'I…'

'There'll be changes,' Max said wearily. 'Starting from the top.'

'If you mean dismissal…' the man said unhappily.

'I'm not talking about dismissal. And, much as my friend over there would like an even more gory fate to befall you, I'm not interested in that either. I want names and ranks, written here.' He motioned to the waiter. 'This man will do it for me. There'll be repercussions, but meanwhile all I have to say is that Levout has no authority to act on my behalf in any capacity whatsoever. Is that clear?'

'That's clear,' he was told unhappily, and he left them writing their names while he returned to Pippa.

'This is a symptom of the mess we need to deal with,' he told her grimly. 'People with friends in high places can order the police force at whim. If you agree that Marc can stay here then I can fix this.'

'Oh, great,' she muttered. 'More blackmail.'

'I'm not blackmailing.'

'Just holding a gun to my head.'

'There are guns to both our heads. You tell me what to do. Brand my mother a liar in public? And surely you don't want to go back to the farm?'

'No, I—'

'And you wouldn't leave the kids here without you.'

She hesitated. Just for a moment she hesitated. 'No,' she said finally. 'Of course I wouldn't. And you know that. Toe-rag.'

'You're calling me a toe-rag?'

'Yes,' she said bluntly. 'I am. You're saying you'll fix this but from a distance? From back in Paris while you build your buildings? I can't take on a proxy role and neither can Marc. If this country is such a mess—'

'I'm doing all I can. Hell, Pippa, until five weeks ago I was a carpenter.'

'And I was a dairy maid,' she said, trying for a smile but not succeeding. Her shoulders sagged. He wanted to…he wanted…

He couldn't. At least he couldn't without speaking to his mother. Hell.

The police were filing out. 'Did you threaten something really messy?' she asked, without much hope.

'No.'

'Just as well,' she said, and tried again to smile. 'I'm not worth it.'

'You are worth it. Pippa, I'm so sorry. You're being sent from humiliation to humiliation. At Tanbarook, and now here.'

'I'm fine.'

'If you stay we have to figure out a role.' Even if he sorted things with his mother—even if he accepted what was starting to seem inevitable—she had to have a place here.

But she was shaking her head. 'Kids' guardian is the only role I want. Me and Dolores can sit in the sun for the rest of our lives. Where's the problem in that?'

'I—'

'Look, let's just organise this damned photo,' she said. 'If it really has to be taken. But I'd rather walk on nails than go back to Daniella's.'

'She's the only decent dress shop in the village.'

'What's that over there?'

She gestured towards the window. People were wandering into what looked like a dilapidated village hall. 'It looks like some sort of repertory company,' she said. 'There are billboards all over the front, and ladies have been going in with dresses.'

'So?'

'So if it's anything like any repertory company I've ever been involved with—'

'You're involved with repertory?'

'I've been Katisha in a Gilbert and Sullivan hospital Christmas pageant.'

The dragon lady in The Mikado? 'I don't believe it,' he said faintly.

'Want to hear an excerpt?'

'No!' Dammit, he wanted to hug her. He hated the bruised look behind her eyes. He wanted…

He couldn't. Hell, he needed to talk to his mother.

She was moving on.

'If this is a repertory company like any I've been involved with they'll have a room full of used costumes out the back. If you get to wear a dress sword, surely I can find something suitable to match.'

The repertory players were fascinated. 'Go right ahead,' they said, laughing among themselves at the thought of the props of their pageantry being used for such an occasion. 'We have costumes here a hundred years old.'

'Excellent,' Pippa said, notably brightening. 'A can-can dancer? Maybe not.'

'We don't usually lend them,' the wardrobe mistress told them. 'We use them over and over again. But for an occasion like this and if it saves you from paying money to that Daniella…'

'She's not popular?' Max queried.

'She's the only business in this town to make money,' the

woman said darkly. 'The rest of us live hand to mouth but Daniella is a friend to the palace.'

That was said with such disdain that both Pippa and Max paused in their search and stared.

'I didn't mean you,' the woman said, flushing a little. 'We have such hopes, Your Highness,' she told Max. 'With you and your family settled in the palace...'

'Just family,' Pippa said. 'Not him.'

'Pippa, leave it,' Max said shortly. 'We came to find you a dress.'

'So we did. Or I did. But I don't need you to help me choose.'

'I'd like to help.'

'Yes, but I don't want you to,' she said, brightness fading. 'I need to get used to working this thing out on my own. Go watch a play rehearsal.'

She emerged a half hour later carrying a really big parcel. She looked pleased, but as she emerged and saw Max waiting for her in the late-afternoon sunshine her smile died.

Why did she stop smiling when she saw him? He didn't like it. 'What did you find?'

'Wait and see.'

Okay. He deserved this. He unfolded his long frame from the stone wall where he'd been sitting. They walked half a block to their car—and Daniella herself came bustling out of her shop to intercept them.

'Your Highness,' she called, and Max paused.

'Get in the car, Pippa.'

'Are you kidding?' She summoned a smile. 'I want to punch her lights out.'

'You're not allowed to punch anyone's lights out.'

'Really?' she said, quasi hopeful.

'Just because you walloped me doesn't mean you can get used to it.'

'No?' She bit her lip, her entrancing twinkle back. 'But I'm really sorry I walloped you.'

'That's fine. It was an entirely justifiable wallop.'

'And walloping Daniella isn't?'

'Not if we don't want a law suit.'

She signed theatrically, but she pinned on a smile as she turned to face the approaching Daniella.

Daniella was in her mid fifties, pencil slim, platinum blonde, dressed in sleek, expensive black. She was clicking hurriedly toward them on six-inch heels.

'I need to apologise,' she said, breathless and passionate, but she spoke only to Max. 'If I'd realised she really had authority—'

'She?'

Daniella motioned to Pippa. 'This woman. You need to get an identification system for authorised servants, Your Highness. The old prince let us know clearly who could buy things on his behalf.'

'Pippa is the guardian of the Crown Prince. She has the royal card.'

'Yes, but she has no money on her own behalf,' the woman said. 'And the little prince is too small to have her in charge. I didn't know what her credit limit was. Let me know and I'll accommodate her.'

'Hello? I'm right here,' Pippa said, but she was ignored.

'Pippa has authority to spend as much as she pleases,' Max snapped.

'The old prince never gave carte blanche to any of his servants.'

'Pippa is not a servant,' he roared, in a voice that startled them all. A toddler, being pushed in a stroller nearby, started to cry.

'What is she, then?' Daniella asked, looking at Pippa as if she were pond scum. Well, she had seen her in her bargain-basement knickers, Pippa conceded. She just knew Daniella wore kinky lace. But she couldn't get a word in edgeways.

'She's Pippa,' Max said through gritted teeth. 'She's part of the new order of things, so you'd better get used to it.'

They were building an audience. The players from the hall emerged as well. They'd obviously watched them leave and the sound of Max's roar had been just too enticing. They were crowding onto the pavement to watch.

'Pippa needs a tiara if she's going to be part of the royal family,' the wardrobe mistress called. 'Come back and I'll find you one.'

'No, thanks,' Pippa called. 'It wouldn't be seemly.'

'Why wouldn't it be seemly?' Max demanded. 'Why can't you have a tiara?'

Pippa blinked, thrown off stride. 'I'd look ridiculous.'

'I'll buy you a tiara.'

'You do that,' the wardrobe mistress called. 'She should have a real tiara. Everyone says she loves the new little prince to bits.'

'But she's not part of the royal family,' Daniella snapped.

'Your part of the royal family is dead and gone,' one of the players called. 'The Levouts' time is finished.' Then, as Max and Pippa looked confused, he explained. 'She's Carver Levout's mistress. She thinks she's royal herself.'

Suddenly the atmosphere was nasty.

'Can we get out of here?' Pippa asked and Max nodded and held the car door open.

'We need to go,' he called. 'Thanks for your help with the dress.'

'Who helped with the dress?' Daniella demanded, white-faced. Maybe she was realising she was missing out on a commission she just might need in the future.

'We did,' the wardrobe mistress called. 'Ooh, it's lovely. She's going to look really royal.'

'Especially beside him,' one of the players added. 'What a hunk.'

'They make a lovely couple,' the wardrobe mistress said mistily. 'A real royal couple.'

'We're leaving,' Max said, revolted, and slipped into the driver's seat beside her. He gunned his little car into life, but they were surrounded by players, smiling and laughing and edging Daniella out of the picture.

'We're so glad you're here,' was the general message, though it came in many shapes and forms.

Max nosed the car forward.

'A real family,' the wardrobe mistress sighed.

'Levout's day is over,' someone else called. 'As of next Friday,' they yelled. 'We're aching to see Levout's face when those documents are finally signed.'

They drove in silence. Pippa stared straight ahead, her face expressionless.

Max was feeling ill.

What was happening here? Why was it such a mess?

He had to get back to Paris.

It had taken him twenty hard years to get where he was now, he thought dully. Some said he'd been lucky, and that was true. His former boss had been a fantastic craftsman and his skills, combined with Max's business acumen, had been a winning combination. But Max had earned his luck. He worked seven days a week, always obliging, always learning, desperate to achieve a fortune in his own right. A fortune that wasn't tainted by royalty.

He'd achieved his aim. He and his former boss had created one of the biggest construction firms in Europe. His mother had one of the finest apartments in Paris and the best of medical care.

None of it was paid for by royal money.

To abandon his career and come back here because of guilt.

No and no and no.

Marc would make a fine prince, he told himself. He and the twins would be happy here.

Only because Pippa would stay with them. Because he was forcing Pippa to stay. He was giving her no choice.

And he had a choice. He'd rejected becoming Crown Prince, but if it would take that look off Pippa's face…

But would she go back to the farm? Would her sense of honour let her stay here?

'What's happening next Friday?' Pippa asked, cutting across his thoughts. 'What documents are being signed?'

He grimaced. He'd meant Pippa to be happily settled in the castle, determined never to revert to poverty, before he set this before her. Why was it suddenly so complicated?

He loved her?

The thought was so incredible that he took his foot off the accelerator for fear of doing something dumb.

Love?

Impossible. He didn't do love.

'Tell me about Friday,' she demanded in a small, cold voice and he forced himself to focus.

Friday.

'The succession has to be decided by next Friday.' Somehow he made his voice free of inflexion. 'The incumbent to the throne has to accept that position within sixty days of Bernard's death.'

'The incumbent. You mean Marc.'

'I guess so. Though you'll have to sign in his stead.'

'Because you won't?'

'I can't sign for him.'

'I mean you won't be Crown Prince.' She brushed her arm across her eyes in a gesture of weariness. 'No. Of course you can't.'

'Pippa, this will be a wonderful life for you.'

'It will,' she said dully. 'I can see that.'

He swore and shoved his foot on the brake. The car stopped dead, right in the middle of the road.

'I hate doing this to you.'

'Sure.'

'No, really.'

'Just leave it, Max.'

'I can't,' he said miserably. 'Hell, Pippa, to drag my mother through such a mess…'

'I can't see that's necessary.'

'I mean figuratively.'

'Oh,' she said flatly. 'Figuratively. I see.'

'You don't see,' he said and he reached out and took her shoulders, turning her so she was forced to meet his gaze. 'My mother was a teenage bride—seduced by my father's looks and money. He got her pregnant. The only reason he married her was that he was in the midst of a row with his own father at the time. Louis wanted him to marry an heiress and he married my mother out of spite.'

'You don't need to tell me this.'

'I need you to understand.'

'I do understand.'

'Pippa, you're gorgeous.'

'Oh, right,' she said and tried to pull away. 'Cut it out.'

'I mean it. Hell, Pippa, all I'm thinking about is you. I'm trying to sort out the succession, the politics, the way the country needs to be structured and all I can think about is you.'

'Then stop thinking about me,' she said angrily. 'You're

making me miserable, and I can't be miserable. I'm going back to the palace to be chirpy like I always am. I'm going back to singing.'

'Like you were in the dairy. To block things out.'

'You're blocking the road.'

'Pippa—'

'You're blocking the road.'

'Dammit, I'm the Prince Regent of Alp d'Estella,' he growled. 'I'm at least the Prince Regent. If I want to block a road then I damn well can.' He glared at her for all of a minute, daring her to gainsay him.

She didn't gainsay him.

'You just sit there looking at me…' he growled.

'What am I supposed to do?'

He knew what he was supposed to do. His path was suddenly crystal-clear.

He kissed her.

He kissed her, and suddenly confusion fell away. Whatever else was wrong in this crazy world, this was right.

She tasted…like Pippa.

Nothing more. Nothing less. He wanted nothing else.

Pippa.

His hands grasped her shoulders so he could pinion her lips right where he wanted them. His mouth claimed hers. For a fraction of a moment she held herself rigid, as if she might pull away—as if she might react with horror, slap him once more?— but it was the sensation of a moment. Nothing more. He felt her resistance slump out of her. He felt her lips open under his.

Pippa.

She was perfection. His hands lowered to her waist and he gathered her close. Dammit, the gear stick was in the way. Why the hell did he have such a tiny car? He was hauling her close, closer and still the damned gear stick was between.

He'd break the thing if he could.

He couldn't. There was no room on her side of the car for him, or his side for her. Outside there was bare bitumen.

He had to make do with what he had. Which was Pippa,

kissing him as he was kissing her. Opening her lips and letting him taste her as deeply as he wanted. Letting his hands hold the curves of her, slip under her T-shirt to feel the silken smooth curve of her bare skin.

He wanted her. He wanted her as he'd never wanted a woman. He wanted her in his bed, and more.

Her hands were in his hair, making him crazy. Of all the erotic sensations... She was deepening the kiss all by herself. Wonderful woman, he thought, amazed by the cleverness of her gesture. Wonderful, wonderful sprite. A red-headed minx who had the knowledge that if she pulled him tighter the kiss couldn't be broken...

He was nuts. He was granting her intellect for one simple gesture. The idea made him smile from within, a great, warming, inward sigh of pure wonder.

Any woman might have done the same, he thought, but there was only one Pippa.

The kiss was endless. Neither of them was willing to break the moment. Maybe if this had been another time, another place, with just a fraction more privacy, without the awful impediment of a gear stick, then they would have taken this further, tumbling into glorious passion.

But they couldn't. They were in the middle of a one-way cliffside road.

Someone was watching.

Max had closed his eyes, savouring the moment. Suddenly some extra sense made him open one eye.

Cautiously.

There were three men and a woman right beside their open sports car. Their audience was watching with every evidence of enjoyment.

'Don't mind us, M'sier,' one of the men said, and he recognised one of the players from the village. 'Our director tells us to study real life. Romain thought we should sound the horn so you could move your vehicle, but, no, I said, one is only young once and maybe we have forgotten. It does no harm to remind ourselves.' He gave a rueful smile. 'The play we are performing, you see,' he said, apologetic but still smiling. 'I play a young man with a young man's passion. Like yourself. But I'm fifty-three years old and I should not be cast as a young man. No matter. All our young have left to try and find work in Italy or France so we are left to do what we can. But it does the heart good to see such reminders.'

Max's eyes were wide open now. As were Pippa's. She was still in his arms but she'd burrowed her head into his shoulder. She choked.

'You laugh and I'll have to kill you,' he whispered.

'Or kiss me again?' she whispered back and he fought to maintain a straight face. Kiss her again? Mmm.

But his audience was waiting for a response. 'I was just comforting Miss—'

'Oh, yes,' the only woman in the group said, understandingly. 'It's very nice that our Prince Regent comforts the guardian of our new Crown Prince. It's a very satisfactory thing to happen. You and this lady? Yes and yes and yes.'

'Levout said at the end of one month you intend to go back to Paris,' the first player told him, settling in for a mid-road chat. 'We asked how is that possible—when the country needs a ruler as much as we do? But of course it's nonsense. Miss will never leave the children. And you…the rumour is that the lady, your mother, was not exactly truthful with your father. All the servants are whispering. Before when we don't see you we accept that she play—how you say—fast and loose. But you… you are a de Gauiter. Yes and yes and yes. So now… This is good.' He grinned. 'This miss will need much comfort. And not in Paris.'

'Hey, I do not need much comfort,' Pippa squeaked, tugging herself away. As much as she could. Which wasn't very far, as Max's arms still held her.

'Miss, if you need to deal with the likes of Levout and his compatriots you will need help,' the woman said. 'He is like an octopus. His tentacles are everywhere. His people will wish you nothing but evil.'

'That's nonsense,' Max said, but he felt suddenly uneasy.

Or more uneasy. These people were verbalising what he already suspected.

And her words were heard and understood by Pippa. 'Let's go home,' she said, no longer laughing. 'Marc—'

'He's fine.'

'Yes, but I want to go home. Please, Max.'

'Sure,' he said and he let her go.

'You keep them all safe,' the woman said.

'This is a wonderful family,' another added. 'We wish you joy.'

'We wish us all joy,' the woman added. 'And maybe it comes true. Maybe it comes true for all of us.'

They drove for the next few minutes in silence. Max stared straight ahead, his mind whirling.

What they'd said was right. He couldn't leave her.

But his mother… His construction company… How could he let them go? And how could he stay here? He'd stay here for what? To keep Pippa safe? And spend the rest of his life in the goldfish bowl as well?

He wanted to pick them all up and take them back to Paris. Be done with the whole sordid mess.

Hell.

'If you grip the steering wheel any harder you'll break it,' Pippa said conversationally, and he eased his grip. A little. With enormous difficulty.

'It's not a great choice, is it?' she said softly.

'No.'

'By Friday next week, you say?'

'Yes.'

'There's a lot of thinking for both of us,' she whispered. 'Meanwhile… Max, please don't kiss me any more. It clouds the issues and we badly don't need clouds.'

The vague sense of unease they'd felt at the player's mention of evil was unfounded. They arrived back as the last of the day's sun played tangerine light on the massive stone walls and turrets, turning the place into more of a fairy-tale setting than it already was. Pascal-Marie, the butler, met them sedately, and Beatrice was close behind. All was well.

'The children have gone to sleep,' Beatrice told them. 'They were too excited to have an afternoon nap. Because the formal photograph session is set for eight tonight, we fed them early and put them to bed. I thought we could wake them at seven.'

'I'll check them,' Pippa said, crossing to the stairway.

'Pippa?' Max called after her and she paused, three stairs up.

'Yes?'

Pippa.

He couldn't think of a thing to say.

'Oh, there is a problem with your dog,' Beatrice added and Pippa stilled. Maybe all wasn't well.

'With Dolores?'

'She's asleep by the fire in the front sitting room,' Beatrice said. 'She romped with the children in the fountain this afternoon. Like a great puppy. We dried her off, and she went to sleep in the sun. It's probably laziness but when the children went up to bed they couldn't persuade her to join them.'

She was through to the sitting room in an instant. Max followed.

The old dog was still sleeping. This room faced south west, with windows all round. Dolores would have had direct sunlight, with the fire adding a little top-up warmth if necessary. The rugs here were inches thick. Why would an old dog move? Max thought appreciatively.

'Dolores,' Pippa whispered and dropped to her knees. The dog opened her eyes, gave her tail a feeble wag and closed her eyes again.

Pippa lifted the old head and cradled it on her lap, running her hand over her flank, letting her fingers lie on her chest. 'Dolores?'

'Is she okay?' Max asked, feeling he was intruding on something personal.

'She's okay,' Pippa whispered, laying her cheek on the old dog's head. 'She's just really, really old, and it'll have been exciting with the children today. The vet told us that this would be her last winter.' She looked up at Max and her eyes glimmered with unshed tears. 'But thanks to you she's had a summer instead of a winter. She has sunbeams and log fires.'

But still that sheen of tears. 'Hey…'

'Could you carry her upstairs for me?'

'To the children's bedroom?'

'I might stay in a room by myself tonight,' she murmured, stroking the dog's soft ears. 'The beds are big but not so big to hold three kids, me *and* Dolores. The kids are feeling safe and happy now, so Dolores and me will sleep next door with the door open.'

Dolores and me. She was sleeping with a dog. Dolores nuzzled against her cheek and he found it within himself to be jealous of a disreputable, ancient Labrador-something.

'Fine,' he managed, neutrally, and he stooped to lift her.

Pippa rose with him, her hands still on the big dog's head.

Dolores' eyes stayed closed.

'She trusts you,' Pippa whispered. 'She knows people, does Dolores. She's never been wrong yet.'

She was too close. The hint of tears in her eyes was damn near his undoing.

Dolores gave a gentle snore, breaking the moment.

'You're sure you want to sleep with her?'

'What's a little snoring between friends?'

What indeed?

He was gazing at Pippa. She was stroking Dolores' ears.

'Let's go,' she said, and he thought, Right, let's go.

He so badly wanted to gather her into his arms. How could he do that with an armful of dog?

It was just as well he couldn't, he thought. What he wanted wasn't…sensible.

So he carried her dog upstairs. Pippa hurried up before him, and by the time he reached the bedroom beside the children's she was spreading a feather-down quilt she'd tugged out of the blanket box.

'That's probably an heirloom,' he said and she put her hands on her hips.

'Well?'

'Nothing,' he said meekly, and set Dolores down.

Dolores opened one eye and her tail gave an infinitesimal wag.

'I'll light the fire,' he said. It was already set in the grate. The room hardly needed heating yet he knew she'd want the dog warm. Besides, it gave him a reason to stay an extra few moments.

'We'll be right,' Pippa said, and walked to the door and held it wide, waiting for him to go. 'Thank you, Max.'

He was being dismissed. She needed a rest, he thought. Or she needed to be alone with her dog.

'Photographs at eight?'

'I'll be there.'

'What about dinner?'

'I'll ask Beatrice to bring something up. I need a nap if I'm going to be beautiful for photos.'

He didn't want to go. She looked so alone. But she was waiting for him to go, glancing sideways at her dog, holding the door wide.

'If there's anything I can do…' he said uselessly and she nodded.

'Thank you. But there isn't. Please, Max, just go.'

Max returned to his bedroom. He paced.

Then he went down to the sitting room Dolores had just vacated. The fire was still burning in the grate. The room was in darkness but he didn't turn the light on.

He paced some more.

'Will you be dressing for dinner, sir?' Blake sounded apologetic, as if he knew he was interrupting serious thought.

'No.' He dragged himself back to the here and now. Blake was standing in the doorway looking worried. 'I'll skip dinner.'

'Cook has prepared roast duck,' he said reproachfully. 'Miss Pippa has said she's not hungry. I believe Cook will be hurt if no one eats her duck.'

Max closed his eyes. Obligations everywhere. Pippa's obligations. His obligations. An obligation to duck.

This one at least he could fulfil.

'Fine. I'll dress and then I'll eat Cook's duck.'

CHAPTER NINE

Max felt ridiculous.

He'd thought the uniform he'd worn the night they arrived was stunning. This one though was even more so. Deep blue and brilliant crimson, it was so startling that when he saw himself in the mirror he started to laugh.

'Sir, it's wonderful,' Blake said with reproach. 'You look so much more handsome than the old prince.'

'I'm only Regent,' he said, staring at the rows of honours on his chest. 'This is crazy.'

'You're our sovereign,' Blake said reproachfully. 'At least until the little prince comes of age.'

Damn the man. He'd had it with the reproach.

'Well, as long as Pippa has something to match,' he growled, thinking of Pippa as he'd last seen her, a waif with tear-filled eyes and an ancient dog. She was as far away from this as it was possible to be.

'Beatrice tells me Pippa's dress is just the solution,' Blake said reassuringly. 'She says it will make us all smile.'

As she'd said, Pippa didn't appear for dinner. He ate in solitary splendour in the grand dining room. Levout was absent as well—which made Max nervous, but he'd rather eat without him than with him. The duck was magnificent. He said all the right things, even though he was having trouble tasting.

He kept thinking of Pippa.

And Dolores. Dammit, he was worrying about a dog.

'Ask Miss Pippa if she'd like us to call a veterinarian,' he told Blake, and Blake looked at him with even more reproach.

'Sir, we asked her that ourselves. She says no, there's nothing wrong with the dog but old age.' He gave a rueful smile. 'There's nothing a veterinarian can do about that.'

'I guess not.' He half rose.

'Chocolate meringues, sir,' the butler said reproachfully. 'And then coffee and liqueur.'

Reproach, reproach, reproach.

So there was no time to return to Pippa's room before the shoot. He made his way to the ballroom as requested at eight.

Beatrice was there, with the three children all rigged out as royal children had been rigged throughout the ages.

'Wow,' he said, astonished. 'You look like something out of Hans Christian Andersen.'

'We look beeyootiful,' Claire said, pirouetting to prove it.

'You've got a sword,' Marc said with deep envy. 'How old do I have to be to have a sword?'

'Twenty-one.'

'But aren't I a Crown Prince?'

'Yes, but I get to carry the sword.'

''Cos Max is the boss of us,' Sophie said, pirouetting with her sister. 'Max fights the baddies.'

'There aren't any baddies,' Beatrice said. 'Let me fix your hair ribbon, Claire.'

'Where's Pippa?' he asked. This was to be the official royal portrait. The photographer—a woman in her seventies—and her two spritely—only sixty if a day—assistants were set up and ready. One of the assistants was approaching him with a palette and brushes.

'What's this?'

'Make-up,' she said. 'So you don't shine.'

'No,' he growled. 'I like shine. Where the hell is Pippa?'

The door swung open.

Pippa.

What the hell…?

This was a transformed Pippa. She was a sugar-plum confection in pink and white and silver. She was a gorgeous apparition that made him blink in disbelief.

Her dress was a floor-length ballgown, with hoops underneath to make it spread wide. Her scalloped neckline was scooped to show a hint of her beautiful breasts. The pink and silver brocade curved in and clung to her waistline, as if the dress had been made for her.

She smiled at them all and twirled in much the same manner as the twins.

She had gossamer wings attached to her shoulder blades.

She was carrying a silver wand.

'Who needs a wish?' she said, and she giggled.

'You're a fairy godmother,' Sophie said, awed, and Pippa chuckled.

'You have it in one. I spent today trying to figure what my role tonight could be. I was feeling a little like Cinderella but then I thought, no, my role is already decided. I'm your godmother. I agreed to bring you guys here—with or without pumpkins—so that's obviously who I am. We have two Prince Charmings and two Sleeping Beauties—' she grinned at the twins '—only you're not asleep any more. So here we are.'

'We could bring Dolores in and she could be the horse,' Marc said, entranced, and a touch of a shadow flitted across Pippa's face. It was so fleeting that Max almost missed it. But he was sure.

'How's—?'

'Dolores really is Sleeping Beauty,' she said, cutting across Max's question. 'You wake her and you'll be the Wicked Witch of the West. Okay, you guys, let's get ourselves photographed.' She twirled again. 'Don't you think this is just the right outfit?'

'No,' Max said, frowning. He was out of his depth here, he thought. But surely Pippa shouldn't be the godmother. What the hell should she be?

Not Cinderella, that was for sure. No maid in tatters, this.

'You look really, really pretty,' Marc said stoutly, casting Max a look of…reproach. *Et tu, Brute?* He dived forward to grab her hand. 'We have to stand right here, Pippa.'

'You look wonderful,' the photographer said, smiling with real appreciation. 'The tabloids will love you to bits.'

'You'll win hearts,' Beatrice said.

Everyone was smiling. Except him.

It felt wrong. Gossamer or not, she didn't feel like a fairy god-mother.

She felt... She felt...

She felt like Pippa.

The shoot lasted over an hour. By then the children were drooping again. Pippa looked exhausted too, Max thought, but she wasn't letting on.

'Enough,' he decreed at last, and the photographer sighed and straightened from her tripod.

'Yes, sir,' she said. 'You're all so photogenic I could keep on for hours. But this will keep the press happy. I'll let the media have whatever they want.'

'Great.' That was why they'd done it. To keep the pressure off. Now they were free of pressure until Friday week.

Then, if Pippa agreed, he'd be free of media pressure for ever.

It should feel good. But now he looked at Pippa's strained face and he thought she'd found this harder than he had. She'd worked at making it cheerful—she was still bouncing, swiping kids with her wand and threatening them with fairy dust if they didn't head straight to bed—but there was something akin to desolation behind the façade.

He'd hauled her out of poverty, he thought, but she knew that riches and glitter weren't enough.

He knew that, too. Could he walk away from this mess? Pick her up and carry her to Paris?

With three kids and a dog?

His mother would adore them.

'Can I help put the kids to bed?' he asked.

'Not tonight.' She carefully didn't look at him. 'And, Beatrice, we don't need you either. We'll be fine. We'll see you in the morning.' She prodded the closest princess with her wand. The princess gave a sleepy giggle and headed bravely to the stairs, fairy godmother in pursuit.

* * *

'Goodnight, sir,' Beatrice said, with all the deference in the world. And then she paused.

'You know, Pippa loves you,' she whispered. 'That has to count for a lot.'

Max stared at her.

How did Beatrice know?

But maybe…maybe…

He wanted to sleep himself, but first he had to front Levout. The official had disappeared for days. He appeared now, standing in the entrance hall, waiting for him, smiling urbanely.

'I believe there was some problem in the village earlier in the evening.'

Max nodded curtly. 'Your friend Daniella.'

'And the players in the town hall.'

'There was no problem with the players.'

'Oh, yes,' Levout said smoothly and he smiled. His smile made Max uneasy. 'There's always been conflict between the people and the palace. I just came to let you know it's sorted.'

'What's sorted?'

'Daniella came to see me, and we've looked into it straight away. We don't like those type of people intimidating our tradesmen and women. These gatherings are clearly inappropriate for our village. So… The hall they've been using is dilapidated. All those tatty costumes in the back are home for vermin. It's surely a safety risk. We've boarded it closed, and in the morning we'll send in bulldozers.'

Max stilled. 'You have no right.'

'We have every right,' he said urbanely. His smile was surface only—behind his eyes was pure venom. 'You might, as Prince Regent, be able to institute changes at parliamentary level, but according to the constitution only a ruling Crown Prince can interfere with daily minutiae. As there will be no ruling Crown Prince for thirteen years we have no problem.'

'A prince has no right to interfere…'

'Exactly.' Levout's oily smile broadened, but underneath there was something akin to hate. 'Which is what I dropped by to tell you. We—the current mayor and our associates—will keep on running the day-to-day affairs of this country as we see fit, regardless of what you do at a higher level. You can return to Paris as you plan and leave it safely to us. Oh, and we don't despair of the future, either. The young prince is already eight years old. By the age of twelve we may be able to persuade him to let things run as generations of monarchs have done before him.' His smile became a sneer. 'What you do, he can be persuaded to undo.'

'Pippa will never allow him—'

'Teenagers revolt,' Levout said softly and smiled. 'Especially if they're encouraged to do so. And Miss Donohue has no authority at all.'

Was Levout right? The lawyers he'd talked to before going to Australia had talked about changing the constitution from an overriding sovereignty to a democracy. They hadn't gone into minutiae.

If Levout was right, it was a mess. For Pippa to cope with it… He couldn't ask it of her. But to walk away…

He had to talk to the lawyers again, he thought. He had to figure out just what Levout and his cronies could really do.

But by next Friday? By the time decisions had to be irretrievably made?

He couldn't leave Pippa.

That was the crux of the matter. The more he thought, the more his mind came back to Pippa. Pippa tonight in her crazy fairy godmother dress, acting as if she hadn't a care in the world, making everyone here smile. Tomorrow she'd make the whole country smile as they woke to their morning newspapers.

His mind stilled, retaining that indelible image of Pippa smiling for the camera.

And the players tonight…

All our young have left to try and find work in Italy or France so we are left to do what we can.

Enough.

He didn't need to contact lawyers.

He went inside to telephone his mother.

* * *

It was two in the morning. He should be asleep, but he'd lain in the moonlight and stared at the ceiling and thought he'd go nuts. Pippa would be asleep. It was crazy to go to her now. She needed to sleep and so did he.

He couldn't.

At three he gave it up for a bad job. He rose and paced to the window. And paused.

There were people on the lawn in front of the castle. The scene was lit by the moonlight. Three figures. One was one long and lean and stooped. One was smaller. Digging? Another figure was a little apart, moving about in the rose bed.

Pippa. And Blake. And Beatrice.

He reached for his clothes and in less than a minute he was out there.

What the hell...?

No one reacted as he came catapulting out the entrance. They kept doing what they were doing. He strode across the lawn, past the fountain and the new decking. Yes, it was Beatrice, snipping roses in the moonlight. Pippa and Blake were digging by the side of the rose garden, just out from the windows of the sitting room.

By the time he reached them he had it figured, and he felt sick.

'Pippa,' he said as he reached them, but she kept right on digging. Blake, however, paused for a breather, resting gratefully on his spade. The ground was dry and hard, Max thought. Blake was too old to be digging.

'Beatrice and I wanted to wake you,' Blake said, sounding relieved. 'But Pippa wouldn't let us.'

'Dolores?' he asked, and Blake nodded.

'She died earlier this evening. Before the photo shoot.'

'Before the photo shoot?' He stared at Pippa, and then muttered an expletive. 'Before the shoot! What the hell do you think you're doing?'

'What does it look like we're doing?' Her voice was laced with tears. 'We have to bury her.'

'Tonight?'

'I don't want the children to see...' She gulped, and wiped her face fiercely with her sleeve. 'They said goodbye to her. When they woke to get dressed for the photographer she was still sleeping, almost normally. But I could feel her heart... It was missing. It was so weak. She could no longer stand, and she was barely conscious. Back home the vet said he'd expected this to happen. Maybe if I'd let you call the vet she could have had a little more time. But she spent today with the children. Beatrice said the children were all over her, exactly as she loves. Then tonight she went to sleep in a sunbeam, by the fire, and you carried her up to my bed. When her breathing got weaker I thought... I thought, for her this day has been perfect. I'm not going to ask her to go on.'

'But you didn't tell the children?'

'The children knew she only had a limited time,' she whispered. 'When they woke for the photo shoot I told them to pop in and say goodnight to her. They all did. I packed her with hot water bottles and tucked her under the duvet. Then, just as I was thinking I couldn't leave her to go to the photo shoot, she just...died.'

'Beatrice knew,' Blake said heavily. 'But Pippa wouldn't let us tell anyone.'

'I didn't want the children to see her dead,' she said fiercely. 'They don't need to. If I thought it would help then, yes, but Marc's had enough death and talk of death. He's old for his years as it is. Tomorrow I want to tell them Dolores died in the night and we buried her here, under her beloved sunbeams. We'll decorate her grave. It'll be sad, but it won't be...'

'It won't be gut-wrenching like burying her is.' Max thought back to Thiérry's funeral. 'No, Pippa,' he said gently. 'You're right. But for you there's no choice but to do the gut-wrenching. How you managed to do the photo shoot...'

'It was the bravest thing we've ever seen,' Blake said, and sniffed. 'She wouldn't let Beatrice tell you...'

'She's my dog,' Pippa said, almost fiercely. 'It's my grief.'

'It's a shared grief,' Max said, and enough, enough. He took the spade from fingers that were suddenly lifeless, and he let it fall as he took her in his arms. He held her close, hard against him, kissing the top of her hair but just holding her. Just holding...

And at last, here they came. The searing sobs that had been so long coming.

Had she cried when her mother died? he wondered. Or Alice? Or Gina and Donald? Somehow he doubted it. All that time she'd been alone, or supporting others.

She'd never be alone again. He made himself that promise, then and there. Never.

There was an ancient stone seat nearby. When the worst of the sobs subsided he lifted her and set her down, beckoning Beatrice and Blake to sit beside her.

'Hold her,' he said to the elderly servants. 'Just sit there, Pippa, and wait. I'm starting what I should have started five weeks ago.'

'Five weeks ago, Your Highness?' Blake queried.

'That's when my mother told me.'

'I wondered,' Blake said softly.

'But you knew?'

'Yes, sir,' Blake said simply. 'The old prince depended on me absolutely. He wouldn't sack me, so I was the only one who was safe. So I was the one she said was your father.' He smiled, misty-eyed in the moonlight. 'May I say, Your Highness, that it would have been an honour. For Beatrice and I, it still is an honour.'

He thought about it while he dug the grave, swiftly and cleanly, using the muscles he'd gained in another life. Then he put such thoughts aside. While Blake and Beatrice cut more roses, he went with Pippa to bring her dog down for burial. He held her hand as they walked upstairs, and she clung as if she needed him.

The big dog lay where she'd died. She looked at peace, Max thought, an old dog at the end of a life well lived, but even so he found himself swallowing hard.

'I don't know what to wrap her in,' Pippa said helplessly, but Max knew.

'Your sweater,' he told her. 'Maybe two of your sweaters, or anything else of yours that you can spare. That's what she'd want to be buried in.' He cupped Pippa's tear-stained face and smiled tenderly into her eyes. 'But she's not a chihuahua. Maybe we'd better add in one of mine for good measure. Dolores was never a one-sweater dog.'

So Dolores was buried, at four in the morning, with all the dignity and reverence they could muster. There were four of them there to say goodbye. Pippa, Max, Blake and Beatrice. Blake and Beatrice took the burial as seriously as Pippa did.

As did Max. It was right. It was a strange little funeral, but lovely for all that. The night was serene and beautiful. The scent of the roses was rich and sweet, and there was an owl calling from the woods nearby.

It was as good a goodbye as was possible, Max thought, and even though Pippa didn't speak he knew she felt the same.

'Come back to bed, sweetheart,' he told her as they finished laying roses over the tumbled earth. 'We'll decorate it properly in the morning.'

'I…' She shook her head, as if trying to shake a dream. 'I don't know…'

'Well, I do,' he said softly and he swept her into his arms and held her tight. 'You're spent, my love. Don't object. Just do what you're told.' And Beatrice and Blake smiled mistily as he carried her inside, up the sweeping staircase, back to her bed.

When they reached the bed the bedclothes were still tousled from Dolores and the fire was still crackling in the grate. He lay her gently on the pillows but her arms were around his neck and she drew him down with her.

'Don't leave,' she whispered.

Leave was the last thing he intended to do. She was cradled against him, soft and warm and lovely. She smelled of the roses she'd held. She tasted of tears. He felt his heart shift within him as he'd never known it could, and, as he stroked her hair, as he kissed her sweet mouth, as he held her close against him, her breasts moulding to his chest, her body curved and suppliant in his arms, he knew that he could never leave.

'Pippa,' he whispered and she held his face in her hands,

kissing him, passive grief slowly fading as passion stirred to take its place.

He kissed her back, the kisses becoming hot and demanding as he felt her response. She wanted him.

Beatrice's words came back to him. 'You know, Pippa loves you.'

Could that be true? Could such a miracle have happened?

Maybe. Maybe.

She was possessive now, her lips claiming his mouth as fiercely as his claimed hers. Her hands were holding his body against hers. Her fingers were feeling the contours of his back, his hips, his thighs.

His fingers slipped under the soft fabric of her T-shirt. She had no bra. Like Max, she'd shed her finery with speed this night, and she'd felt no need to dress in more than a cursory manner.

Her breasts were moulded to his hands. Her nipples were taut under his fingers. He breathed out, a soft sigh of sensory pleasure, of acceptance that this miracle could somehow be happening, that this woman could possibly be his.

Maybe she did love him, he thought exultantly. She loves me before I've promised her a thing. She loves me despite what I've been trying to make her do.

And somehow it made the world right. His world, which had been torn apart when Thiérry was killed, or even earlier, when his mother had lied, when his parents' marriage had fractured, was somehow settling back on its rightful axis. Love conquered all. It does, he thought exultantly. Damn the critics, the cynical. He had his Pippa. He'd found love.

'Pippa.'

The word was an echo of his thoughts. For a moment he didn't react, thinking it was just a part of this night.

But he felt Pippa still in his arms. She put her hands up to his hair and let her fingers run through, as if somehow imparting a message that this had to be interrupted. Her name wasn't part of the night. She was being called.

The outside world was slipping in.

Reluctantly he loosened his hold and she twisted in his arms. He could barely see her in the firelight, but the night-light was on in the sitting room and the slight figure in the doorway was unmistakable. It was a little boy in too-big pyjamas, his voice wavering toward panic. 'Pippa?'

'Marc.' Pippa was out from his arms, rolling off the bed, crossing to fold the little boy into her arms. 'Marc, what is it?'

'Who…who's there?'

'I'm here,' Max said gruffly, trying to make his voice sound normal. 'I was just…'

'Max was giving me a cuddle,' Pippa said. 'Did you hear us? Did we scare you?'

'No.' He faltered, looking towards the bed. Max flicked on the bedside lamp, thanking his lucky stars that Marc hadn't waited for another five minutes. For if he had…

'Where's Dolores?' Marc whispered and the night stilled. 'I woke up and you weren't with us. And I thought about Dolores. Where's Dolores? I was just…scared.'

'She's dead, Marc,' Pippa said, hugging him close. She was stooped to his level, hugging him against her, and the sight was enough to make Max feel…feel… Hell, he didn't know what he felt. He'd spent his whole life avoiding relationships and now here he was, in the midst of so many relationships he didn't know where to start.

But Pippa seemed too choked up to talk. The responsibility was suddenly his. 'Dolores died peacefully in her sleep,' he told Marc, and Marc looked over Pippa's shoulder and met his gaze head-on. 'That's why I'm here hugging Pippa.'

'Really?'

'Really.'

'Where is she?' He gazed fearfully around the room, and Max thought, yes, Pippa had been right to speed the burial. Sometimes children needed to be involved in all things, but not this time. Not when Marc's grief for his parents was still raw.

'Pippa and I buried her,' Max said.

'Where?'

'Just below these windows. Near the rose garden.'

'In the moonlight,' Pippa whispered. 'And where the sun shines all day.'

Marc swallowed. 'I should... I should have helped,' he said and damn, Max was as close to crying as he'd been for years. This waif of a child was squaring his shoulders like a man. He was under no illusion that Marc would have used the spade if he'd had to.

'You know, you can't see the grave from here,' he said, crossing to the windows and looking out. 'It's too dark. Would you like to come down and see what we've done?'

Marc considered. 'Yes,' he said at last. 'Please.'

'You should be asleep,' Pippa said ruefully, but Max shook his head.

'No. He needs to see the grave. Will you come with me?' He held out his hand to Marc.

'Yes.'

'I'll come, too,' Pippa said, but Max caught her shoulders and forced her to turn to him.

'No,' he said softly and he kissed her, softly, tenderly, as she needed to be kissed. 'You're dead tired, my love. You've cared for Dolores. You've cared for all of us. Now it's time for the men of the family to take care of you. Marc, Dolores was Pippa's dog for a long time, much longer than you or I have known her. She's feeling very sad. And she's tired. Will you tuck Pippa into bed while I fill hot water bottles?'

'Okay,' Marc said, cautious but game. 'Pippa, you have to get into bed.'

'But I—'

'Don't argue with us,' Max said firmly. 'We're in charge. You know, Marc and I have some serious talking to do, too, and it's a good time for us to do it now, when all the womenfolk are asleep. So, Pippa. Bed.'

'Bed,' said Marc.

She stared at them for a long moment. Prince Regent. Crown Prince. Her men, giving orders.

She smiled wearily at them both and she went to bed.

She didn't sleep, but, safe under the covers, warmed by the fire and by the hot-water bottles Max had filled, she felt as at peace as she'd ever felt in her life.

Dolores' death was a grief but not an overwhelming one. She'd known this was coming, and for it to happen in this way was a blessing. She knew it. And now… She'd thought she'd be bereft, but she wasn't.

For things had changed. Max was no longer looking at her as if she was some sort of trap.

She was no longer alone.

She wasn't sure of the whys or wherefores, but she let her thoughts drift where they willed, content to let tomorrow take care of itself. Somewhere downstairs Max was having a heart-to-heart talk with Marc. What about? Maybe she should be in on the conversation, but she trusted Max.

She trusted him with her life.

She rolled over and one of her hot-water bottles slid out on the floor. No matter. She didn't need it.

But Max had given it to her. For some dumb reason it seemed important to retrieve.

She slid out from under the covers and groped in the darkness until she found it. She went to climb back into bed, but, almost as an afterthought, she crossed to the window.

And saw…

Max and Marc were on the seat she'd so recently vacated. They were talking steadily. Max's arm was around Marc's shoulders. She blinked.

And then she looked at the grave.

For she could see the grave now. No longer a darkened mound in a darkened garden, it was an oasis of light.

The boys—the men, she corrected herself—had brought out candles. They'd found tea-light candles, many candles.

There was a perimeter of candles around the grave. And then, among the roses, the candles spelled out letters.

DOLORES.

Where had they found so many candles?

No matter. She could see the colours of the roses, illuminated by the candles. She could almost imagine she could smell them. The grave looked wonderful

Beside the grave, Max and Marc spoke earnestly on.

She blinked and blinked again but she didn't cry. The time for crying was over.

She hugged her hot-water bottle to her. Max wouldn't come back to her this night, she knew. She didn't need him to.

Tomorrow was just...tomorrow.

CHAPTER TEN

PIPPA woke and sun was streaming in the window. Her door was wide open, and the children were filing in.

They were dressed and washed and sparkling, the twins' pigtails plaited, neat as pins, and full of importance.

Sophie was bearing a glass of orange juice.

Claire was carrying a plate of fruit.

Marc was balancing a tray holding toast, pots of jam and a tub of butter curls.

Max was bringing up the rear, carrying coffee.

'Good morning,' he said, and her heart felt as if it did a somersault. 'Or almost good afternoon.'

She stared at the clock. Eleven!

'We let you sleep in,' Sophie said. ''Cos you were up in the night looking after Dolores.'

'Oh, Sophie…'

'I told them Dolores died,' Marc said, matter-of-factly. 'We've put more flowers on her grave. Sophie put pansies on and Claire chose pretty white flowers with yellow middles. They'll die pretty soon but Max says we'll all go for a drive later to a garden place. We'll each choose what we want to plant on Dolores' grave. And Max said we can light the candles every night for as long as we want.'

'That's…that's lovely.'

'But you need to get up,' Claire said importantly. ''Cos we have a visitor.'

'Who?'

'Sort of a grandma,' Sophie said and she giggled.

'She says we can call her Grandma, anyway.' Marc sounded a bit uncertain. 'But she says only if you think it's okay.'

'Who is it?' Pippa asked, intrigued.

'My mother,' Max said.

She blinked.

'And she's waiting for you to wheel her round the garden,' he told the kids. 'Use the ramp at the side door and don't take her anywhere the wheelchair can get stuck.'

'We won't,' Sophie said and dumped her orange juice and ran. Closely followed by Claire.

'And I'm not going to be Crown Prince any more,' Marc added, setting down his toast with care. 'Max and me talked about it last night and we have a plan. It's really good. But can I go and help wheeling? They might crash the wheelchair if I don't.'

'Go right ahead,' Max said, placing his hand on the boy's thin shoulder and giving him a squeeze of affection. 'You're a kid in a million.'

Marc gave a self-conscious grin, smiled shyly up at his hero—and bolted.

Pippa was left with Max. She should feel shy too, she thought. She didn't. She just felt…right.

'How soon is soon enough to ask you to marry me?' Max said, and her world stilled.

'What did you say?'

'You heard.' He set down the coffee pot on the floor. 'I was intending to wait until you'd eaten your toast, but you're far too beautiful to leave hanging around for long. Someone else might snatch you.'

'I have three kids,' she said, trying hard to keep breathing. Her heart was doing really funny lurching things. 'No one else wants to snatch me.'

'More fool them,' he said and sat on the bed and pulled her into his arms. 'They don't know what they're missing. I have the most wonderful woman in the world in my arms right now. How fantastic is that? I can't believe my luck and I'm waiting not a minute longer. You need to say you'll marry me, my lovely Pippa. You must. Please?'

Her heart was singing, but somehow she found the strength to pull away. He released her with seeming reluctance, but he did let her go.

She pulled far enough back until she could see his face. 'Max, why?'

'I love you.' He smiled, that lovely, lurking smile that had her heart doing hand springs. 'As simple as that. As easy as that. All the conniving I've done—the figuring, the way I've tried to structure our lives—and in the end it comes down to this. I love you, Pippa, and I love you with all my heart. I want to be beside you for as long as we both shall live. Everything else has to come in after that. We'll organise our lives. We'll organise the Crown and the country. But we'll organise these things around the most important thing in my life. Which is being with you.'

She didn't answer. She couldn't. She'd surely forgotten how to breathe.

'Say you'll marry me,' he said, urgently. 'Pippa, I'm not asking you to step away from the children. I know you love them to bits, and, believe it or not, I do too. I thought last night how could I walk away from Marc? There's been so many things to think about. For the last few weeks it's been crazy. First it was how I could accept that I was truly a de Gautier. Then could I walk away from this country? After that how could I walk away from you? And now there's the kids, worming their way into my heart. I love them too, Pippa, I love this whole damned catastrophe. I want to marry the lot of you.'

'And take us to Paris?' It had to be said. She was torn between disbelief and a magic, wondrous hope.

'No, here's the thing,' he said ruefully. 'Because I can't do that either. I listened to those elderly players yesterday saying their kids were having to leave the country. I thought about fractured families. I thought about this wonderful little country that can be so much if it's well managed. And I thought about the buildings I've been proud constructing. Yes, I can be proud of my buildings but here… Pippa, here we can build a whole country.'

'But how…?'

'There's so much we can do,' he said, exultant. 'The people

who talked to me initially in Paris—disaffected citizens who are aching to be allowed to set decent government in motion—are desperate to help, and they will. If I stay on as Crown Prince…'

'You'd take that on?'

'Yes,' he said firmly. 'It's not fair to ask that of Marc. It never was, but it's taken the love of a wonderful woman to make me see it.' He grinned. 'And also to see that it might not be so much a burden as a privilege. I've talked to Mama. She's agreed—with sadness but I'll make her see it need not be a grief. We'll set the DNA testing in place to prove things. But you know what? I've been thinking and thinking. I thought it'd be great if Marc stands to inherit. I talked to him about it last night and he agrees. So… We can formally adopt. The kids will be our kids, along with whoever else comes along. That way it's Marc who stands to inherit. How perfect is that?'

'But…' It was too much to take in. 'You love them that much?'

'I love them so much I can't do anything else,' he said, and he tugged her into his arms and held her tight. 'Pippa, last night I rang my mother in Paris. Like me, her life has been desolate since Thiérry died. We've put things on hold. But last night I talked to her about what we can do—what we all can do—if we have the courage to take this on.'

'You've really asked her to…'

'Yes,' he said, stroking her hair, kissing the top of her head. 'Yes, I did. I told her that once upon a time I remembered her talking of a vision she had of how this country could be. She married as a green girl, marrying the fairy tale. I told her we could live the real fairy tale. We could make this country great. And we could be a family.'

'Your mother…' She was finding it hard to get her mouth to form words.

'You'll love her,' he said, urgently, putting her away from him a little so he could make her see. 'She's a wonderful, wonderful woman and she'll love you to bits. You'll love her to bits. She's nervous now, but she's brave enough to want to try, and she's already falling for the children. She'll help us, Pippa. There's no way one person can be sovereign in this country. We need a family.' He hesitated. 'But there is one problem.'

'Only one?'

'She has a dog,' he said, rueful. 'A weird-looking mutt called Hannibal she saved from the street several years ago. She has him here.'

'She brought her dog?'

'I rang her last night and talked this all through with her,' Max confessed. 'Before I'd finished talking, she was organising plane tickets. She and Hannibal flew into Monaco at dawn and she hired a car to bring her here. She's ready to be part of this, and so is her disreputable mutt. But, Pippa, it's asking a lot of you. You'll have three kids, a husband, a mother-in-law, a castle full of devoted retainers and a maniac dog whose sole desire in life is to destroy every shoe he ever sets eyes on. Beatrice says as far as she knows there's never been a dog in this palace, and now it's looking like Dolores might have been the start of a dynasty.'

His grip on her hands grew urgent. 'I've thought it all through. All night… There's been so much to think of. We could donate the kids' farm to be the wildlife corridor you were so enthusiastic about. Maybe we could keep the house so we could visit every now and then—but not in midwinter. It'd almost be worth the plane fare to tell the Tanbarook supermarket ladies ourselves.'

He hesitated, waiting for her to smile. Waiting for her to say something. Nothing came.

'But is it too much, do you think?' He held her shoulders, desperately anxious. 'Do you think you can take it on?'

'I…'

'And your nursing,' he added, figuring he had to set all the facts before her before she refused or accepted. 'There's a hospital in the village. There's been no young nurses in the place for years and it's really run-down. I thought maybe you could take it on as your special project. There are more hospitals through the country. So much to do. And me… As soon as we've finished Blake's house we'll move on to rebuilding the village hall. I've had to move fast to stop demolition this morning and that's only the beginning. There's so much. We'll make this country the greatest of the Alp Quartet. Raoul thinks he's done well in Alp d'Azuri. He doesn't know the half of what great can be.'

'Hush,' Pippa said, half laughing, half crying. 'Max, do you know what you're saying?'

'I surely do.' He paused, his smile fading as their gazes locked. The plans fell away. There was only this moment. This man, and this woman.

'Pippa, will you take us on?' he whispered. 'I know you haven't been born into it. I know you can walk away. But we need you so much. Will you wave your wand, my wondrous fairy godmother? Will you marry me?'

She smiled at him, her eyes misting with unshed tears. Her Maxsim, Crown Prince of Alp d'Estella. Her own true love.

Would she marry him? How could she not?

And it was a first.

'I never heard it said that any fairy godmother got to marry Prince Charming herself,' she whispered, drawing him into her and holding him close. 'But there's always a first, my love. Move over, Cinderella. Yes, my lovely prince. My Max. My love. Yes, I will.'

* * * * *

Mediterranean Nights

Join the guests and crew of Alexandra's Dream, *the newest luxury ship to set sail on the romantic Mediterranean, as they experience the glamorous world of cruising.*

A new Harlequin continuity series begins in June 2007 with FROM RUSSIA, WITH LOVE *by Ingrid Weaver*

Marina Artamova books a cabin on the luxurious cruise ship Alexandra's Dream, *when she finds out that her orphaned nephew and his adoptive father are aboard. She's determined to be reunited with the boy...but the romantic ambience of the ship and her undeniable attraction to a man she considers her enemy are about to interfere with her quest!*

Turn the page for a sneak preview!

Piraeus, Greece

"THERE SHE IS, Stefan. *Alexandra's Dream*." David Anderson squatted beside his new son and pointed at the dark blue hull that towered above the pier. The cruise ship was a majestic sight, twelve decks high and as long as a city block. A circle of silver and gold stars, the logo of the Liberty Cruise Line, gleamed from the swept-back smokestack. Like some legendary sea creature born for the water, the ship emanated power from every sleek curve—even at rest it held the promise of motion. "That's going to be our home for the next ten days."

The child beside him remained silent, his cheeks working in and out as he sucked furiously on his thumb. Hair so blond it appeared white ruffled against his forehead in the harbor breeze. The baby-sweet scent unique to the very young mingled with the tang of the sea.

"Ship," David said. "Uh, *parakhod*."

From beneath his bangs, Stefan looked at the *Alexandra's Dream*. Although he didn't release his thumb, the corners of his mouth tightened with the beginning of a smile.

David grinned. That was Stefan's first smile this afternoon, one of only two since they had left the orphanage yesterday. It was probably because of the boat—according to the orphanage staff, the boy loved boats, which was the main reason David had decided to book this cruise. Then again, there was a strong possibility the smile could have been a reaction to David's attempt at pocket-dictionary Russian. Whatever the cause, it was a good start.

The liaison from the adoption agency had claimed that Stefan had been taught some English, but David had yet to see evidence of it. David continued to speak, positive his son would understand his tone even if he couldn't grasp the words. "This is her maiden voyage. Her first trip, just like this is our first trip, and that makes it special." He motioned toward the stage that had been set up on the pier beneath the ship's bow. "That's why everyone's celebrating."

The ship's official christening ceremony had been held the day before and had been a closed affair, with only the cruise-line executives and VIP guests invited, but the stage hadn't yet been disassembled. Banners bearing the blue and white of the Greek flag of the ship's owner, as well as the Liberty circle of stars logo, draped the edges of the platform. In the center, a group of musicians and a dance troupe dressed in traditional white folk costumes performed for the benefit of the *Alexandra's Dream*'s first passengers. Their audience was in a festive mood, snapping their fingers in time to the music while the dancers twirled and wove through their steps.

David bobbed his head to the rhythm of the mandolins. They were playing a folk tune that seemed vaguely familiar, possibly from a movie he'd seen. He hummed a few notes. "Catchy melody, isn't it?"

Stefan turned his gaze on David. His eyes were a striking shade of blue, as cool and pale as a winter horizon and far too solemn for a child not yet five. Still, the smile that hovered at the corners of his mouth persisted. He moved his head with the music, mirroring David's motion.

David gave a silent cheer at the interaction. Hopefully, this cruise would provide countless opportunities for more. "Hey, good for you," he said. "Do you like the music?"

The child's eyes sparked. He withdrew his thumb with a pop. *"Moozika!"*

"Music. Right!" David held out his hand. "Come on, let's go closer so we can watch the dancers."

Stefan grasped David's hand quickly, as if he feared it would be withdrawn. In an instant his budding smile was replaced by a look close to panic.

Did he remember the car accident that had killed his parents? It would be a mercy if he didn't. As far as David knew, Stefan had never spoken of it to anyone. Whatever he had seen had made him run so far from the crash that the police hadn't found him until the next day. The event had traumatized him to the extent that he hadn't uttered a word until his fifth week at the orphanage. Even now he seldom talked.

David sat back on his heels and brushed the hair from Stefan's forehead. That solemn, too-old gaze locked with his, and for an instant, David felt as if he looked back in time at an image of himself thirty years ago.

He didn't need to speak the same language to understand exactly how this boy felt. He knew what it meant to be alone and powerless among strangers, trying to be brave and tough but wishing with every fiber of his being for a place to belong, to be safe, and most of all for someone to love him....

He knew in his heart he would be a good parent to Stefan. It was why he had never considered halting the adoption process after Ellie had left him. He hadn't balked when he'd learned of the recent claim by Stefan's spinster aunt, either; the absentee relative had shown up too late for her case to be considered. The adoption was meant to be. He and this child already shared a bond that went deeper than paperwork or legalities.

A seagull screeched overhead, making Stefan start and press closer to David.

"That's my boy," David murmured. He swallowed hard, struck by the simple truth of what he had just said.

That's my *boy*.

"I CAN'T BE PATIENT, RUDOLPH. I'm not going to stand by and watch my nephew get ripped from his country and his roots to live on the other side of the world."

Rudolph hissed out a slow breath. "Marina, I don't like the sound of that. What are you planning?"

"I'm going to talk some sense into this American kidnapper."

"No. Absolutely not. No offence, but diplomacy is not your strong suit."

"Diplomacy be damned. Their ship's due to sail at five o'clock."

"Then you wouldn't have an opportunity to speak with him even if his lawyer agreed to a meeting."

"I'll have ten days of opportunities, Rudolph, since I plan to be on board that ship."

* * * * *

Follow Marina and David as they join forces to uncover the reason behind little Stefan's unusual silence, and the secret behind the death of his parents....

Look for From Russia, With Love by Ingrid Weaver in stores June 2007.

HARLEQUIN®

Mediterranean NIGHTS™

Tycoon Elias Stamos is launching his newest luxury cruise ship from his home port in Greece. But someone from his past is eager to expose old secrets and to see the Stamos empire crumble.

Mediterranean Nights
launches in June 2007 with...

FROM RUSSIA, WITH LOVE
by *Ingrid Weaver*

Join the guests and crew of *Alexandra's Dream* as they are drawn into a world of glamour, romance and intrigue in this new 12-book series.

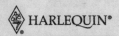

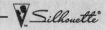

SPECIAL EDITION™

COMING IN JUNE

HER LAST FIRST DATE

by *USA TODAY* bestsellling author

SUSAN MALLERY

After one too many bad dates, Crissy Phillips
finally swore off men. Recently widowed,
pediatrician Josh Daniels can't risk losing his
heart. With an intense attraction pulling them
together, will their fear keep them apart?
Or will one wild night change everything...?

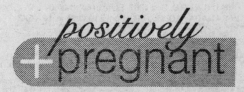

**Sometimes the unexpected
is the best news of all....**

REQUEST YOUR FREE BOOKS!

2 FREE NOVELS PLUS 2
FREE GIFTS!

HARLEQUIN ROMANCE®

From the Heart, For the Heart

YES! Please send me 2 FREE Harlequin Romance® novels and my 2 FREE gifts. After receiving them, if I don't wish to receive any more books, I can return the shipping statement marked "cancel." If I don't cancel, I will receive 4 brand-new novels every month and be billed just $3.57 per book in the U.S., or $4.05 per book in Canada, plus 25¢ shipping and handling per book and applicable taxes, if any*. That's a savings of over 15% off the cover price! I understand that accepting the 2 free books and gifts places me under no obligation to buy anything. I can always return a shipment and cancel at any time. Even if I never buy another book from Harlequin, the two free books and gifts are mine to keep forever.

114 HDN EEV7 314 HDN EEWK

Name	(PLEASE PRINT)	
Address		Apt.
City	State/Prov.	Zip/Postal Code

Signature (if under 18, a parent or guardian must sign)

Mail to the **Harlequin Reader Service®**:
IN U.S.A.: P.O. Box 1867, Buffalo, NY 14240-1867
IN CANADA: P.O. Box 609, Fort Erie, Ontario L2A 5X3

Not valid to current Harlequin Romance subscribers.

Want to try two free books from another line?
Call 1-800-873-8635 or visit www.morefreebooks.com.

* Terms and prices subject to change without notice. NY residents add applicable sales tax. Canadian residents will be charged applicable provincial taxes and GST. This offer is limited to one order per household. All orders subject to approval. Credit or debit balances in a customer's account(s) may be offset by any other outstanding balance owed by or to the customer. Please allow 4 to 6 weeks for delivery.

Your Privacy: Harlequin is committed to protecting your privacy. Our Privacy Policy is available online at www.eHarlequin.com or upon request from the Reader Service. From time to time we make our lists of customers available to reputable firms who may have a product or service of interest to you. If you would prefer we not share your name and address, please check here. ☐

HR07

HARLEQUIN *Romance*

Coming Next Month

#3955 A MOTHER FOR THE TYCOON'S CHILD Patricia Thayer
Rocky Mountain Brides

Dedicated Mayor Morgan Keenan has no time for love. It takes newcomer tycoon and caring single father Justin Hilliard to see past Morgan's defenses and help heal her painful past. Can Justin show Morgan that she's meant to be his adored wife and a mother?

#3956 THE BOSS AND HIS SECRETARY Jessica Steele

When Taryn Webster takes a job with gorgeous millionaire Jake Nash, she is determined not to mix business and pleasure. But then Jake asks her for help out of hours! At first Taryn refuses, but she can't resist his persuasive arguments—nor his charming smile and tempting gray eyes.

#3957 THE SHEIKH'S CONTRACT BRIDE Teresa Southwick
Brothers of Bha'Khar

Sheikh Malik Hourani, Crown Prince of Bha'Khar, is a rich and powerful man, dedicated to ruling his kingdom—but experience has made him wary of love. Beautiful Beth Farrar has been betrothed to the sheikh since birth, but she has a secret! She's not the woman he thinks she is.

#3958 MARRIED BY MORNING Shirley Jump
Makeover Bride & Groom

When playboy Carter Matthews decides to prove his reliability by getting married, his ever-practical employee Daphne thinks his idea is ridiculous. Especially when she discovers that she's his chosen bride-to-be! Will Carter and Daphne be married by morning?

#3959 BILLIONAIRE ON HER DOORSTEP Ally Blake

Billionaire Tom Campbell is content with his pace of life in sleepy Sorrento. Then he walks up to the doorstep of Maggie Bryce's ramshackle mansion, and he can see both are in need of some loving care. Maggie's alluring mystique captures the billionaire's heart and he can't let go.

#3960 PRINCESS AUSTRALIA Nicola Marsh
By Royal Appointment

Natasha Telford is an everyday Australian girl. Dante Andretti is gorgeous, charming...and a prince! They couldn't be more different. But Dante needs her help and Natasha is just the ordinary girl he's looking for. Maybe she has what it takes to be his extraordinary princess!

HRCNM0507